THE SPIRIT OF THE LAW ♣ BOOK THREE

THE THIEF OF THE LOST TREASURE

LIZ HEDGECOCK

Copyright © Liz Hedgecock, 2024

All rights reserved. Apart from any use permitted under UK copyright law, no part of this publication may be reproduced, stored in a retrieval system, or transmitted, in any form or by any means, electronic, mechanical, photocopying, recording or otherwise, without the prior written permission of the copyright owner.

This is a work of fiction. Names, characters, businesses, places, events and incidents are either the products of the author's imagination or used in a fictitious manner. Any resemblance to actual persons, living or dead, or actual events is purely coincidental.

ISBN-13: 979-8332936852

*For the cartographers and mapmakers,
who lay out the past and present for us*

CHAPTER 1

Spring was in the air as I patrolled the mean streets of Liverpool. The mild streets, really, since there was nothing doing. No new graffiti or other signs of vandalism, no overturned bins, no suspicious gatherings on street corners. Members of the public only spoke to me to say hi. Mostly it was 'Hi, Constable Saunders' – though a few cheeky ones called me Tasha. Lord knows how they'd got hold of that, unless they'd heard Steph and me chatting in the lunch queue at the kebab shop.

Anyway, nature was turning over a new leaf, as far as it could in the middle of a city. No shows of snowdrops or daffs here, as there would be in Sefton Park, but the tufts of grass which had forced their way through the concrete were fresh and green, and there was a patch of blue in the sky. All in all, it felt as if the year was moving on.

And things were moving on at Erskine Street

police station, too. For one thing, Steph and I were spending a lot more time there. The Chief was on one of his crackdowns about efficiency and proper use of the budget, and having two constables spend half their time in a disused police station didn't exactly fit with that.

So our presence at the Bridewell, formerly a necessity for at least half of every working day, was down to three hours a week: Monday, Wednesday, and Friday, twelve till one. The budget had run to a laminated notice for the Bridewell's door, telling any callers outside those hours to ring or visit Erskine Street. That was understandable. In all the hours I'd spent at the Bridewell, we'd never had one member of the public call in. However, the Bridewell wasn't just a disused police station. It was the home of Merseyside Police's longest-serving officers, Nora Norris and Superintendent Hicks.

I hadn't learnt the Bridewell's secret until late last year, under very strange circumstances. Now I knew, though, it was impossible to see the Bridewell as I had before. And Nora and Superintendent Hicks, frankly, were a right pair.

I completed my beat for the morning and strolled back to Erskine Street. The temptation to do another round and call it diligence was strong, since when I got in Sergeant Doughty would probably find something tedious for me to do. He was even worse than usual at the moment, because Sergeant Jones – Huw to all of us – had escaped for two weeks in the Caribbean, the lucky so-and-so. I had the date of Huw's return marked on my calendar and believe me, I was counting the days.

I walked into the police station and, as no members of the public were about, took off my hat. 'Eleven o'clock and all's well,' I said to Sam, who was on the desk.

'You lucky swine, Tasha,' she said. 'Doughty's got me looking through traffic offences for the last five years. No idea why.'

'Pointless busywork?'

'Oh yes, that'll be it.'

'Fancy a brew? It must be my turn for a round.'

Sam brightened a little. 'Oh yes. A nice strong coffee might kickstart my work ethic. Or not.' She scowled at her computer screen.

I entered the main office. Heads were down, and a thick cloud of gloom and boredom hung in the air.

I went to the corner desk. 'Nothing untoward to report, sir,' I said, with a smile.

Sergeant Doughty looked up and the left corner of his mouth twitched. 'Thank you, Constable Saunders. I take it you have things to get on with.'

'Oh yes, sir.' I fought the impulse to salute, which would probably have been taking things too far. It wasn't that I respected Doughty particularly, more that for some reason I was on his good side. And I planned to stay there. 'Would you like a drink?'

'Tea, three sugars,' he said, and returned to whatever he was reading.

'Right you are, sir,' I said, and performed a smart about-turn before he asked why I was still there. 'I'll assume everyone wants a brew, unless you say otherwise,' I announced to the office, and received several thumbs up in reply. Not from Steph, though. Her head was bent over a document and she was muttering to herself.

I headed to the kitchen and began the ritual of the brews. Mugs lined up according to the list on the drinks-cupboard door. *I'm the Boss* mug for the sergeant, *You don't have to be mad to work here but it helps* mug for Sam, a Snoopy mug for me, a generic mug for Steph, whose usual mug, red with white polka dots, was still at the Bridewell. Fill the kettle. Teabags, instant coffee, sugar where appropriate. Two biscuits each on a side plate: Bourbons this week. And now we wait.

Yes, Steph and I were seeing a lot more of each other these days. Not so much at work, where, though she was present in body, she was generally glued to something Sergeant Doughty had dumped on her. I was spending a lot more time at her flat. I had a toothbrush there, and a set of PJs, and toiletries. Those drove Steph bananas. 'How can one person use so much . . . stuff?' she asked as she tried, not for the first time, to fit all my bits and pieces in the bathroom cabinet.

'I'm not exactly low maintenance, Steph,' I replied, shaking my head so that my hair rippled over my shoulders. I swear she used to think I woke up like this.

'Yes, but... What is skin food? And . . . brightening serum?'

'Necessities,' I said firmly. 'One of these days I'll give you a facial, then you'll understand.'

Steph actually shuddered. 'What I understand now is why you've never moved out of your mum's and got your own place. Your beauty regime won't let you.'

'Mum likes having me around,' I said. 'It's as easy to cook for two as for one and I pay my share of the bills. Maybe you should move in with us.' I laughed. 'You wouldn't need more than a couple of suitcases.' I surveyed Steph's bare flat, which she called minimalist.

I could see her holding in another shudder. 'I like my own space,' she replied.

Which was true. Even when we were together, sometimes Steph seemed to retreat into a secret place in her own mind, where she fretted. I could understand why, as Sergeant Doughty often made remarks about *everyone* needing to pull their weight in these difficult times, and he was usually standing by Steph's desk when he said it.

All in all, it felt as if Steph's arrival at Erskine Street almost six months ago belonged to a bygone age. Then, things had been as carefree as they can be when you work in a city police force. Now our noses were kept to the grindstone, since Inspector Farnsworth was mostly invisible, either out at meetings or shut in his office, and the day-to-day running of the show was down to the two sergeants. And Doughty, who'd been a sergeant way longer than Huw and could quote *Blackstone's* chapter and verse, always got his own way.

I made the drinks, put them on the battered Cains Brewery tray, and took them round the office. Thanks were muttered, biscuits taken, and quiet resumed.

I delivered Steph's drink to her coaster. 'Thanks,' she murmured, without looking up.

I put down her biscuit plate and retreated to my desk across the aisle. I had a report to finish which would see me nicely through to lunchtime. I took papers from my in-tray and arranged them on my desk, more for effect than from necessity. It was important to look busy, or Sergeant Doughty would make sure you were. Even if you *were* busy, that wouldn't stop him giving you extra. As Steph knew. She and I rarely left at the same time when we were on shift together, since she was usually wrestling with a task that had landed on her nice tidy desk during her lunch break or while she was on the beat. I'd learnt that lesson early on and had a considerably lighter workload as a result.

I was nearing the bottom of the page and wondering how to sum up when the Addams Family theme tune rang out beside me. Steph silenced her phone quickly, but not before a huff from the corner of the room.

'Bridewell time?' I asked.

'Yup,' said Steph. 'And as always, I'm in the middle of something.' Her short hair was at odd angles from running her hands through it as she read, and she seemed ruffled. Ruffled, and worried.

'I can go if you like,' I said. 'Let me print the report I'm working on, and I can figure out the conclusion while I'm down there.'

'You see, Constable Sharpe?' Doughty remarked from the corner. 'Multitasking.' I had no idea why he was so hard on Steph, but if I could do anything to help her, I would.

'Would you mind?' Steph's brow was furrowed, her mouth downturned, her shoulders tense. I'd have given her a massage if we hadn't been in the office. 'I'll lose the thread if I stop.'

'Not a problem.'

'Say hi to Nora for me. I missed her on Monday.'

'Sure.' I hit *Print*, fetched the keys from their hook in the key cupboard, popped a couple of pens in a folder and put on my hat. To be honest, the Bridewell was a much easier ride than Erskine Street. I could hang out in the yard with Nora and the superintendent, ask them about the old days, which they loved, and drink as much tea as I wanted. It was kind of like visiting your grandparents. If your grandparents were ghosts, which mine weren't.

I collected my printout, stuck it in the folder and headed off, signing out at the desk on the way.

'Off again?' said Sam, rolling her eyes.

'Bridewell duty,' I replied. 'You know how it is.'

'Don't envy you that,' said Sam, who despite her hours clocked in at the Bridewell had never met Nora or the superintendent. I hadn't either until things got strange.

'Don't worry,' I told her, 'I'll keep myself amused.' And with that, I headed into the thin winter sunshine.

CHAPTER 2

I unlocked the great door of the Bridewell and stepped inside. The first thing I did was pick up the *OPEN* sign which lived in the rack by the door and swap it for the *THE BRIDEWELL IS CURRENTLY CLOSED* sign. Once that was done, I closed the door behind me. Only then did I call 'Hello? Anyone home?'

Silence.

That wasn't altogether unusual. Nora and the superintendent spent a lot of time in the yard, keeping the ghosts of the police horses company and, in the case of Superintendent Hicks, having a crafty smoke. Not that anyone's lungs would be damaged now, but it was the principle of the thing. Got to stay within the law.

The yard, however, was empty, apart from the two faint horses standing in the corner, presumably where their stables had been. 'Hello, you two,' I said, wishing I had a ghost carrot for them. 'Don't suppose you know where the others are?'

The stout black one, who Nora called Queen Victoria, harrumphed and shook her head. 'I'll take that as a no.'

Next, I went to the file room in the basement. I couldn't see the appeal, since the ghosts couldn't open the cabinets or take out files, but they liked to chill in there. Today, though, the room was empty, apart from dust dancing in the pale rays of light which had battled through the grimy window.

Where else could they be? I was so busy puzzling over their absence that I only saw the hole in the floor of the corridor when I was nearly in it. I dodged it, muttering a word which Nora would definitely have told me off for if she'd been anywhere near.

I climbed the rickety stairs, giving them close attention, but the ghosts were still very much in my mind.

Next I tried the detective offices upstairs, but all I found was a mug Steph had forgotten, whose contents were growing a thin layer of mould, and doodles on the top page of the notepad: stars outlined over and over again, growing larger and larger until they were poking each other with their spiky points. I wondered what a psychiatrist would have made of it, and decided I was better off not knowing.

At least I could deal with the mug. I took it

downstairs and washed it in the icy water which was all the Bridewell offered. *Where can they be?*

Then a thought occurred to me. *What if I can't see them any more?*

All at once, I felt empty. Had I lost the ability? But I could still see the horses, and the human ghosts were usually much clearer to me, since I'd spent a lot more time with them.

Could they be hiding? Why? They were usually delighted to spend time with someone different, catch up on gossip, maybe read a magazine or a newspaper while I was there to turn pages for them. I knew Inspector Farnsworth took them to the Athenaeum Club one evening a week to read ghost books and chat to Mr Chapman, the very long-serving librarian, but that was hardly a full social life.

One explanation remained. I could barely allow myself to think it. *What if they've gone to their rest?* Had they somehow done whatever it was they'd been left on earth to do, and passed on to the afterlife? I'd seen it happen – not once, but twice. I wasn't sure whether to be glad or sorry. Surely the afterlife would be better for them, but though I'd known them only a short while, I would miss them both terribly.

Now, of course, I remembered what Steph had said about missing Nora on her last visit. What if I had to break the news to Steph that our ghostly colleagues had gone for good? Inspector Farnsworth would be upset, too.

I hurried from room to room, calling them. I even unlocked the cells and looked within, although why anyone would hole up in those cold, echoing places was beyond me.

No ghosts anywhere.

My breath was quick and shallow. *They can't be gone*, I told myself.

They can.

But I don't want them to be! I pushed my hair off my forehead and realised I was sweating. Sweating, in February.

I ran my finger round the inside of my collar. *I need air.*

I ran into the yard and stood in the middle of it, gasping and dizzy. I bent and put my hands on my thighs, trying to slow my breathing.

'Are you all right, Constable Saunders?'

I shot upright so fast that I nearly fell over. Superintendent Hicks, dapper as ever, was coming down the iron staircase from his quarters at the top of the building.

'I thought you'd both gone!' I cried.

'Us, gone? What could make you think a silly thing like that?' He was patting his pockets for his pipe and looking about him.

'I called you both and you didn't answer.'

'Ah. Busy. We must not have heard you.'

'I really shouted. You usually tell me I'm too loud.'

'Well, I'm here now. Forgot it was a visiting day. One day is much like another in here.' He paused. 'Anyway, enough of our plight. What did you want?'

I studied the superintendent. He wore an irritated expression, which was normal for him, but he wouldn't meet my eye. He hadn't from the moment I saw him.

'Superintendent…'

'Yes, Constable Saunders?' His eyes met mine and his gaze slid away.

'Where's Nora?'

'She's busy too. Um, in my quarters.'

'Your quarters? What's she doing up there?' As far as I knew, Nora wasn't allowed in Superintendent Hicks's rooms. The superintendent was keen to maintain his considerable seniority, even though Nora was his only companion most of the time. I imagine he welcomed a rest from Nora, who could be pretty full on.

'Never you mind,' said the superintendent, drawing himself up. 'It is not a constable's duty to poke their nose into other people's business.'

I grinned, and whistled. Not that I thought the pair of them were up to anything of a romantic nature – that didn't bear thinking about. However, I figured that teasing the superintendent might draw out the truth.

'I shall not be baited, Constable Saunders. Especially by an inferior.'

I smiled. 'You do realise there's nothing to stop me going up those stairs and seeing for myself?'

'How dare you!' the superintendent shouted. 'You, a junior officer, threatening to violate the dignity of a helpless spirit!' He stood, glaring at me. Even his moustache was bristling with barely suppressed rage. 'The next time I see Inspector Farnsworth, you'll be for it.'

'OK, I'm sorry,' I said. I wasn't too worried about his threat, since I was prepared to bet that the matter would be forgotten by the time Inspector Farnsworth met up with the ghosts again. Besides, I suspected the superintendent's outrage was intended to throw me off the scent of whatever they were up to.

I watched the superintendent cool down. He still wouldn't look at me properly. Then his gaze travelled over my right shoulder and his eyes widened.

I whipped round. Nora was frozen in the doorway. 'There you are!' I exclaimed. 'Where have you been?'

'Oh, um, doing ghost things.'

'Obviously. What sort of ghost things? I've been hunting for you two everywhere.' I turned to Superintendent Hicks. 'You told me Nora was in your quarters.'

'She has been,' said the superintendent. 'All

morning. She, er, went to visit the bathroom.'

'Nora never does that,' I said. 'She can't use it.'

'I went for old times' sake,' said Nora, removing her hat and smoothing her reddish-gold hair. 'I do that sometimes with rooms I don't need any more. So I don't forget.'

I didn't believe a word of it.

'Well, I'm going to my quarters,' the superintendent announced, and turned to ascend the stairs.

'Weren't you coming down for a smoke?'

He stopped and faced me. 'I was, but after the abuse I received just now I've gone off the idea. I'm going where I won't be disturbed or insulted.' He went up, his feet noiseless on the treads, until he vanished through the door at the top.

'And then there was one,' I said, facing Nora. 'Seriously, have you been up to something?'

'How would I do that?' said Nora. Her face was a picture of innocence. 'I don't have any special powers. I can't leave the station, not unless I'm on police business, and it isn't as if you or Steph spend enough time here to find new cases for us to investigate.'

'I'm sorry,' I said, and meant it. 'I'd spend more time here if I could, but Steph and I have to toe the line. The Chief's put his foot down, and Sergeant Doughty is enforcing it. He's having a great time. The rest of us, not so much.'

'I'm sorry too,' said Nora. 'I've been on the receiving end of harsh discipline.' She glanced at the superintendent's quarters. 'It's just hard for us, though we can't expect the Chief to understand.'

A wave of sympathy rushed through me. How awful to be stuck in one place, unable to meet anyone new or do pretty much anything, and have your main diversion taken away. 'I'll see what I can do, Nora,' I said. 'I can't promise anything, but I'll try to speak to the inspector. He's on our side.'

'I know,' said Nora. Suddenly, her woebegone demeanour lifted and she regarded me with a speculative eye. 'Can you help me with something, Tasha?'

I looked at my watch. 'Yes, if I can do it in the next five minutes. That's when consultation hour ends and I have to return to the station. Doughty's probably got his stopwatch out, ready to time my return.'

Nora pouted. 'This will take longer than that.'

'In that case, you should have been here when I arrived. Then I could have helped.'

'Five minutes,' she said, bitterly. 'You wait until you've got all the time in the world and nothing to do with it.'

That made me shiver. 'That's pretty harsh, Nora. It's not my fault you're here.'

'It's your fault that you won't help me,' said Nora. 'What am I supposed to do now?'

'Can't the superintendent do it, whatever it is?'

'No. It needs a human. A live human.'

'It'll have to wait till Friday. I'll let Steph know, then we'll both be prepared for whatever it is.'

'Huh.' Nora folded her arms. 'What if it can't wait?'

My phone alarm went off. 'Time's up,' I said. 'Gotta go.' In truth, while I was sorry for them both, I was also annoyed that they'd messed me around. And despite their genuine anger and irritation, I had a definite sense that they were up to something. How that could be, I had no idea. 'Bye, you two,' I called, loud enough for the superintendent to hear, but received no acknowledgement.

Fine, I thought. *Be like that.* I went in and began the process of locking up. *So much for an easy time at the Bridewell. I'll be glad to get back to Erskine Street. Maybe.*

CHAPTER 3

It was my turn on the front desk that afternoon. That suited me fine. I liked talking to members of the public, even if it was just signposting them to the local Citizens' Advice Bureau or telling them where they could get their shoes mended. Sometimes, of course, it was more serious. And I took it seriously. My face was the first one they saw, and it was up to me to make sure they felt they would be listened to.

And being on the desk also meant that I wasn't in the main office. Sergeant Doughty kept, I swear, a drawer full of mundane tasks which he saved specially for whoever was doing time out front. However, tedious as they always were, we knew he wouldn't come and dump more stuff on us. For someone who had presumably joined the police to help people, the sergeant wasn't too fussed about meeting them. I suspected most of the locals didn't know his name. But he must have been in a good mood that afternoon, as he merely said, 'I trust you have things to be getting on with, Constable Saunders,' and left it at that.

I wasn't going to argue. 'Yes, sir,' I said, and took off sharpish.

It was an afternoon of bits and pieces. New graffiti on the end wall of a shop, a smashed headlight, youths loitering on a street corner. One old dear came in to say that someone had strung a pair of trainers over one of the phone cables in her street. 'You know what that means,' she said, darkly.

'I'll get it looked into,' I said. 'Can you give me the street name and postcode, and I'll pass the details on.'

'Thanks, love,' she said, and went on her way shaking her head, possibly at the wickedness of the world.

When my phone buzzed at four thirty, I thought it might be a text from Steph. Considering we sat in the same office, we'd barely managed to exchange more than a few words that day. However, when I fished my phone out of my pocket, the display said *Mum*.

I clicked on the message.

Will you be home tonight? I'm making lasagne.

That was my favourite. Mum knew exactly what she was doing. And to be fair, I hadn't been home since the weekend, when I'd dropped off some washing.

I checked the waiting area. No one was watching.

I could be, I typed. *I'll check with Steph.* I pressed *Send,* then started a new message. *Are we doing anything tonight? Mum asked if I'd be home for tea.*

I put the phone away and returned to updating the log. I was just considering how to describe the trainer alert when my pocket vibrated. *That was surprisingly quick.*

Mum again. *I meant to say that Steph is very welcome too, if she wants to come.*

I'll tell her, I replied, and relayed the message. As I pressed *Send*, I saw Steph hadn't read the last one yet. *I'll give her half an hour*, I thought.

Really, though, I already knew that Steph wouldn't see my message. She hardly ever looked at her phone in work time. She was absolutely paranoid about Sergeant Doughty catching her out. 'I'm getting towards the end of my six-month probation period here,' she said. 'If I can stay out of trouble till then, I'll be able to relax. I don't know what I'd do if I got sent back to Cheshire.'

I didn't know what I'd do, either. Cheshire was less than an hour's drive, but it felt a world away. 'It's not just up to Sergeant Doughty,' I told her. 'Inspector Farnsworth's in charge. You're still in credit from sorting out that business at the Athenaeum, anyway.'

'Better safe than sorry,' said Steph, and addressed herself to her screen again.

I would never have said it to her face, but all work and no play made Steph a dull girl. She was too tired to go out after work, usually, and lunch breaks together were a rarity now. Today I'd gone to the kebab shop on my own, feeling like a right Billy No Mates as no one else was free. I brought a chicken special back for Steph, half of which was still there an hour later, with bits of lettuce wilting on the plate. She hadn't touched the Snickers bar, either.

So, after half an hour, I texted Mum to say that I'd see her later and messaged Steph that I was going to Mum's for tea.

Finishing time crawled round and I returned to the main office. On the way, I checked my messages. Steph still hadn't read hers.

'The end of another exciting day,' I said. 'I'm off to Mum's.'

'Uh huh,' said Steph, still reading. The more she read, the more there was to read, like in that old cartoon with the brooms that keep doubling.

'Have you thought any more about what I said?'

Steph tore herself away from her screen. 'What's that?'

I glanced around. Everyone was either wrapped up in what they were doing or getting ready to leave. 'You know,' I murmured. 'Nora and the super.'

Steph looked blank. Then comprehension dawned. 'Oh, yeah. Dunno.'

'They were both acting funny. As if they were hiding something.'

Steph frowned. 'What can they have to hide? They can't do anything. Besides, if another ghost turned up at the Bridewell, or one of them got exciting new powers, they'd never be able to keep quiet.'

'That's what worries me,' I said. 'What if it's something serious and they feel they can't tell us?'

Steph gave me a warning glance. I suspected Sergeant Doughty's antennae were wiggling. 'OK,' I said, 'I'll bear that in mind. See you.'

'Night,' said Steph. She'd already turned back to her screen.

I felt lighter as soon as I stepped out of Erskine Street. I nipped to the flat to get changed and pick up a shirt which had lost a button, then headed for Liverpool Central. By the time I got off the train at St Michael's, I was practically floating. I got some funny looks – a woman strolling along, grinning to herself – but I didn't mind.

I reached Mum's house, spick and span in the middle of a row of terraces, and let myself in. 'Mum, I'm home!'

'In the kitchen,' she called. 'Now you're here, I'll put the lasagne in.'

'Smashing.' I wandered through and gave her a hug. 'How many are you feeding?' I asked, inspecting the lasagne.

'Well, I wasn't sure whether Steph was coming, and you'll probably want to take some back with you. The rest can go in the freezer.'

'Fair enough,' I said. 'I did text you that Steph couldn't make it.'

Mum shrugged. 'I hoped she might change her mind. Anyway, let's stop wasting energy and get this in the oven.'

I showered while Mum pottered about. When I came downstairs, she held up my shirt. 'All done. Didn't you see the spare button by the washing label?'

I giggled. 'Never even looked.'

Mum clucked her tongue at me. 'You girls – I mean you young women nowadays. I hope Steph knows how many beans make five, because you don't.'

'Steph's a workaholic,' I said, checking the water level in the kettle and switching it on. 'That button would have to make an appointment with her two weeks in advance.'

Mum laughed. 'That's a bit mean, Tash.' Then her smile disappeared. 'Are you two all right?'

'I guess.' I got my special mug from the cupboard. It said *Natasha* on it in fancy script. I'd thought of taking it to Steph's, but it didn't feel right somehow. Mum's mug was bone china with pink roses on. 'She's working a lot at the moment.'

'You always say that,' said Mum. 'Should you be

working harder?'

'I do work hard,' I said. 'I do my hours. What more can they want? I'm allowed to have a social life.'

'I know, but these are difficult times. Cost of living, and budget, and . . . stuff.' Mum and Dad, bless them, had worked in the public sector in the days of strong unions and great pensions. Dad had passed three years ago – dropped dead of a heart attack – but Mum was comfortably off and could haggle like a demon. 'Are you managing?' She looked concerned. 'I've got a bit put by this month, if you need—'

'We're fine for money, Mum.' Not as fine as I'd like to be, but we could manage. 'It's just – it's been a funny day. A couple of my colleagues were being a bit odd.'

'In what way?' The kettle pinged. Mum took down the teapot and poured in hot water. 'You never remember to warm it.'

'Sorry. They were a bit shifty, as if they were hiding something, but I don't know what they could be hiding. They don't have the power to do anything.'

'So they're juniors.' Mum got the teabags. 'Are they normally good colleagues?'

'Yeah. Yeah, they are.'

'In that case, I wouldn't worry. If they do want you to get involved in any funny business, just say no. Maybe warn them that you'll report them if it carries on.'

'Maybe.' I couldn't help smiling at the idea of reporting the funny business of two ghosts to Sergeant Doughty, who'd probably have me committed. 'Thanks, Mum, you're a star.'

'Yes, I am. And so are you.' Mum pulled me in for a hug and I felt myself relax. 'Now, let's get this tea made and see what's on the telly.'

We watched rubbish, ate lasagne and Mum filled me in on the local gossip. The goings-on of Nora and the superintendent seemed to be part of another world entirely. Occasionally I thought guiltily of Steph, who was probably eating a microwave meal, watching something mindless and fretting about work. But she seemed a long way away, too.

CHAPTER 4

Mum woke me with a cup of tea at seven. 'Rise and shine, love,' she said. 'If you get yourself in the shower now, you'll have time for a bacon sandwich before you go. All your uniforms are pressed. And I popped an emergency Snickers bar in your bag.'

I stretched. 'Aw Mum, you're the best.'

I actually got to work early for once. But Steph was earlier, sitting alone in the middle of the office and scrolling through yet more documentation. Even Sergeant Doughty wasn't in, unless he was hiding in one of the filing cabinets. 'Morning,' I said. 'What are you reading?' I'd have kissed her, but she didn't seem in the mood for that sort of thing.

'Witness statements for a hit and run. No serious injuries, luckily.' She looked me up and down. 'You're very bright-eyed and bushy-tailed.'

'I slept like a log.' Steph was bleary-eyed, but not in the manner of someone who'd had a good night's sleep. More like someone who'd been up half the night. 'Oh, and my mum's given me enough leftover lasagne for both of us tonight.'

'That's nice of her,' said Steph, sounding indifferent. 'Say thanks from me.'

'Will do.' I studied Steph. She didn't seem cross exactly, but she wasn't pleased to see me, either. Mind you, if I'd been stressed at work and she'd gone off to be pampered by her mum, maybe I wouldn't have been pleased with her. Not that it had ever happened. I decided an olive branch was in order. 'Would you like a brew?'

'Please.' Steph frowned at her screen. 'I wonder if I need an eye test.'

I found myself whistling as I walked to the kitchen, and stopped. Then I started again. It wasn't my fault that I was cheerful. *Steph should relax more*, I thought, as I pulled the kitchen door open. What I saw nearly made me let go of it. 'What the—'

Nora was standing in the corner. 'Hello,' she said, looking guilty as all get out.

'What the heck are you doing in our kitchen?' I demanded. 'How did you get here?'

'I walked,' said Nora. 'It isn't far from the Bridewell.'

'I know that!' I realised I was almost shouting and lowered my voice. I couldn't risk someone walking in on me having a conversation with what would look like empty air. 'I thought you couldn't leave the Bridewell unless you were on police business. So why are you here?'

'I had to talk to someone,' said Nora. 'Someone alive, and it couldn't wait till Friday.'

I walked to the kettle and flicked it on. I definitely needed a brew now. 'Right, let's start from the beginning. How did you get here?' I spoke slowly, enunciating my syllables precisely, as if Nora was slightly hard of hearing.

Nora fidgeted. 'I got Superintendent Hicks to give me an order.'

'You what?' I stared at her.

She seemed relieved to have got the truth out. 'I don't know why we didn't think of it before. We can only leave the Bridewell on police business – but if the superintendent gives me an order to go somewhere, that's police business, isn't it?'

'I suppose it is.' I got two mugs and dropped teabags in them. Snoopy looked sceptical about the whole situation.

'I miss tea,' said Nora, gazing longingly at the mugs. 'Made properly, with tea leaves in a Brown Betty teapot, though. Not with those funny little paper bag things.'

'Each to their own,' I replied.

'If you'd used tea leaves, I could have told you your fortune. I used to be good at that.'

'Oh, really? I can tell fortunes, too.'

Nora raised her eyebrows. 'Can you?'

'Yep. Your fortune is that you'll be in a heap of trouble if you don't tell me what's going on right now.'

'I'm trying to!' cried Nora. 'You're the one who keeps wanting silly details, like how I got here.'

She had a point. 'Sorry,' I said. 'It's just that you gave me a shock.'

The kettle was working itself up to a boil and I used the time to take deep breaths and calm myself. Once I'd poured water in the cups, I faced Nora again. 'So why *are* you here? I assume it's not for a fun day out. More of a busman's holiday.'

'I wish it was a fun day out,' said Nora, gloomily. 'I haven't had a moment's peace.'

Not another one, I thought. 'What's the matter, Nora?'

'I saw a ghost,' said Nora.

I nearly laughed. Then I realised Nora looked rather scared. 'What sort of ghost, and where? At the Bridewell?'

'In my head,' said Nora. 'Sort of like a dream, if I ever slept.'

I imagined Nora seeing something spooky in the dead of night, and shivered. 'Go on.'

'I first saw her wandering on some grass and she seemed so sad. She was in a plain brown dress, with her hair loose, and her feet were bare. "Where is my baby?" she cried. "Where is my treasure?" I tried to talk to her, but she kept walking away. "I do not want *you*, with your official buttons," she said. "Perhaps you took him." And she kept wandering and calling.'

'Oh no,' I said. I would have given Nora a hug if I could.

'She faded after a few minutes and I hoped that was the last of it. Some sort of strange nightmare. But she came back the next evening. She still wouldn't talk to me, but this time I followed her and saw flowerbeds, like in a park, and lots of people wearing modern clothes. Those big swollen coats with the furry collars.'

'Puffer jackets.'

'Yes, those things. And they had torches and they were shining them around. "Where are you?" they were saying. "Come out, come out, wherever you are!"'

'So they were helping?'

'No. The woman hurried away from them, muttering "I cannot let them find me! Or are they hunting for my little treasure? To keep him for themselves?" She started weeping, then she disappeared. But the next night, she returned.'

'What happened then?'

'The other people were still there, calling and shining the torches about. This time, instead of following her, I followed them. When I looked up, I saw the pillars of Central Library and knew exactly where I was. Not in a park, but St John's Gardens, right by St George's Hall in the city centre.'

'Yes, I know it,' I said. 'Why was she searching for her baby there, though?'

'I didn't understand that either,' said Nora. 'But the next morning, I told Superintendent Hicks what I'd seen and he said that before the hall, there was a hospital. And a cemetery.'

'Well I never. I suppose that makes sense, then.' I tried to get my head around what Nora had told me. 'Why has she come to you in a vision if she doesn't want your help? Who are the other people?'

'That's what I wondered. So I asked the superintendent to send me to St John's Gardens. He was suspicious, and said it might not be safe, but I persuaded him.'

'Why didn't he come with you?' *Typical*, I thought. Men sending women into places they didn't think were safe.

'He couldn't, could he? He's the most senior person at the Bridewell, so no one can order him to do anything. And we didn't know if it really was police business or not. Besides, someone's got to mind the Bridewell.'

'Hmm.' It sounded a bit too convenient to me. 'So you went to the gardens?'

'I did. The people were there. Not with torches, as it was daytime, but they were holding up little black boxes with red lights on and waving them around. The black boxes reminded me of Steph's fake ghost detector.'

'Steph's what? Oh, never mind. Go on.'

'I was a bit worried because I thought they might see me, but none of them did. That meant I could get up close. They were saying things like "Need to get in the hall for a proper look" and "I can definitely feel something. Maybe it's here." I moved off then.'

'Did you see the woman?'

Nora shook her head. 'They probably scared her away.'

'Right.' I realised the teabags had been brewing for some time and fished them out. 'So what do you want?'

Nora gave me a surprised glance.

'I mean, I assume you haven't come all the way here to tell me a creepy story.'

'Of course not! I want you to come to the gardens with me.'

'Me? Not Steph?'

'I don't think Steph can see more than two inches in front of her nose at the moment,' said Nora. 'I need help, Tasha, and you're my best chance.'

I got milk from the fridge and topped up the tea. It was so strong that I had to tip some out to make a normal-coloured brew. 'OK, when?'

'Can we go now? I mean, when you've had your tea. Not right away.'

'I can't just leave,' I said. 'Being a police officer doesn't work like that, as you know.'

'You seem to be able to come and go when it suits you,' Nora replied, in a sulky tone.

'I wish. It may seem that way to you, but I assure you my days are pretty full.' *Not as full as Steph's, but I'm better at playing the system.*

I thought it over. 'OK, here's the deal. Because I was in early, I might be able to take a longer lunch. If you come back at quarter past twelve and put yourself somewhere inconspicuous, I'll get out as soon as I can. It won't give us long, but it's better than nothing.'

Nora looked relieved. 'Thank you, Tasha. I don't know what's going on at St John's Gardens or St George's Hall, but I don't like it. Not one bit.' She walked towards the door, then turned. 'Will you tell Steph?'

'Maybe.' I felt bad about keeping a secret from her, especially since I thought of Nora and Superintendent Hicks as Steph's ghosts, but on the other hand, it was exciting to be going on a mission of my own. 'I'll see how I feel. She probably won't be free at lunch anyway.'

'I know that,' said Nora. 'But maybe you should tell her, just in case.'

'I'll think it over,' I said, picking up the drinks. 'See you later.' It was only when I delivered Steph's drink and sat down at my own desk that I thought, *What does she mean, just in case?*

CHAPTER 5

I'd like to say that the hours dragged until my rendezvous with Nora, but the morning was unusually busy. Within a few minutes of returning to my desk, Sergeant Doughty was hovering like an officious ferret. 'Constable Saunders, are you doing anything that can't wait?'

'Not really, sir,' I said, glancing at my in-tray.

'Good. A witness to a mugging is coming in to give a statement shortly, and I want you to sit in.'

'Yes, sir. Thank you, sir.' I could feel Steph rolling her eyes, even though she was obscured by the sergeant. Was it my fault that sometimes I got asked to do things she fancied? I'd been at Erskine Street longer – I'd been a police officer longer. It was perfectly fair. If Steph didn't always look as if she was drowning in work, maybe she'd get more chances like this. 'Shall I take notes, sir?'

'We'll be recording it.'

'Oh. OK, sir.'

'Might need you to make brews,' he said, and went to his desk.

When I turned to Steph, her face was hidden by her hand. I felt as if I was doing the wrong thing just by existing. It certainly wasn't a good time to tell her about Nora. For one thing, the sarge could return any minute. Besides, I wasn't sure what her reaction would be – particularly to the information that Nora had asked me and not her – so I left it.

The taking of the statement was something and nothing. 'You won't need to do any talking, Constable,' said Sergeant Doughty. 'I'll introduce you, of course, but I'll be asking the questions.'

I was required to make drinks, but otherwise I was free to form my own opinion of how Sergeant Doughty was handling things. I wasn't impressed. He didn't put the witness at her ease, and didn't ask what I thought were the obvious questions. Instead, the witness grew more and more flustered as he questioned her on minor details until she sat silent on the plastic chair. Finally, she burst out 'But I saw it, I know I did.'

'We'll leave it there,' said Sergeant Doughty. 'Interview ended at half past nine,' he said, to the recorder. 'Constable, clear these cups while I complete the formalities, then escort the witness to reception.'

'The sergeant's a detail man,' I told her, as we walked along the corridor. 'It isn't personal.'

'It felt personal,' she said, bitterly. 'I wish I hadn't bothered to come in.'

'It's good that you did,' I said, 'and your account of what happened was fine.'

'I hope you catch them,' she said, and walked out before I could thank her for her time.

Noon came round quickly. The hour was marked by Sergeant Doughty getting up from his desk. 'I have a meeting with Inspector Farnsworth and the Chief,' he announced generally. *The largely invisible Inspector Farnsworth*, I thought. 'No shirking, now.' And off he went.

This was my chance. Knowing how the Chief could go on, I figured I'd be safe for at least an hour. 'I'm nipping out a bit early,' I told Steph. 'See you later.' I was gone before she had a chance to reply. And yes, I did feel guilty.

I borrowed a coat from lost property to hide my uniform and found Nora loitering in an alcove near the front desk. 'There you are!' she cried. 'I've been waiting ages.'

'Give over, Nora, I'm early,' I said. 'I'll sign out, then we'll get going.' I checked the time on my watch, which was always at least five minutes fast, and added a couple more minutes to my signing-out time in case it had righted itself.

The walk to St John's Gardens was, shall we say, an experience. Nora dodged between pedestrians, skulking behind lamp posts and using litter bins as cover, then darting forward. If I hadn't known her, I'd have arrested her for being a public nuisance. I tried to ignore her and walk as quickly as I could without marching or looking official.

'What are you doing?' I muttered, as she hurried past.

She turned and put her hands on her hips. 'Have you ever been walked through?' she asked, then yelped as someone did that very thing.

'Oh. Carry on, then. I'll see you at the main entrance to the gardens.'

She saluted, and made another dash for it.

I reached the gardens first and looked among the flowerbeds for a woman fitting Nora's description. There were a few small groups, dressed for the weather and deep in conversation, but no sign of a woman in a brown dress with bare feet. *What if I can't see her?*

Nora arrived, panting. 'Do you have to go at such a pace?'

'Yes, if I want to make it back to work on time. Can you see her?'

Nora peered. 'Not from here. She was near the hall last time.'

We climbed the slope, glancing this way and that

as the hall loomed ahead, but everyone was in modern dress and generally wearing big boots. 'Don't tell me I've come all this way for nothing,' I muttered. 'And I'm hungry.'

'There!' Nora pointed dramatically.

Sitting on the steps of Gladstone's statue, hugging her knees, was a small, slender woman in dingy brown. 'Go and speak to her,' said Nora.

'I'm going!' I tried to seem casual as I made for the statue. The woman hadn't noticed me, though. She appeared lost in her thoughts. 'Um, excuse me?'

She jumped, then gazed up at me. I don't know what she was expecting, but she seemed relieved.

'Sorry, I didn't mean to startle you. Are you all right?'

'I am cold,' she said, 'but I am always cold. And I am tired, but I am always that, too. Thank you for your kind enquiry.' Her voice was high-pitched and thin, like a supporting character from a period drama. She could have been anywhere from sixteen to thirty, but she looked chilled to the bone. Her skin was so pale it had a blue tinge, and her lips were the purple of a fresh bruise. I suspected the poor woman had frozen to death while out searching for her baby.

'I wondered if I could help.' It was killing me to be so vague, but I couldn't risk her thinking I was in cahoots with Nora.

She beckoned me closer. 'Don't tell them I am

here,' she whispered, a conspiratorial gleam in her eye.

'I won't,' I said, and sat down beside her.

'Why are you wearing trousers?' she asked. 'I see many ladies in them, but I never had a chance to ask one before.'

'Well, they're practical and warm.' She gazed lovingly at my uniform pants. 'Who do you mean by *them*?'

'Don't you know?' She stared at me, but now her expression was amused, not frightened. 'The attendants. Matron commands them and she is not a kind lady. Not at all. In fact' – she leaned closer – '*I* would not call her a lady.'

'Do you mean the staff at the hospital? Are you – are you unwell?'

'I am perfectly well, but when I tell people that, they laugh. I cannot be at a hospital, because Mama and Papa would summon a doctor if I required medical attention. That is what they did when I was unwell every morning and the doctor told me I must rest. And again, when I had pains in my...' She leaned closer. 'My *stomach*,' she whispered, and giggled. 'Then I gave birth to my sweet baby. When I came round afterwards, from a lovely sleep, they told me he was being cared for in a special place and sent me in a coach to visit him. That is how I came here: but I found only strangers. The attendants brought me food but it wasn't very nice, and when I asked where my baby was they said there was no baby and I must be mistaken. But I know there was a baby. I remember. That is why I went to search for him.' She looked up at me. 'Have you seen him? A beautiful child, with such a lusty cry.'

'I . . . um, I'm not sure.' I could feel my cheeks burning. 'Could you tell me what year it is? I seem to have forgotten.'

She laughed. 'What does it matter?'

'It might be important,' I said, hoping I was doing better than Sergeant Doughty, and not sure that I was.

Her forehead wrinkled. 'I was born on the twenty-fourth of March, 1795, and when I left to visit my baby everyone was terribly worried about the war. That rascal Napoleon!'

'Oh, I see.' My historical knowledge wasn't great, but I had a distinct feeling that I'd have to go further back than Queen Victoria. Had this woman lived in Jane Austen's time, maybe? I studied her dress for clues, but it was plain and shapeless. 'Could you tell me your name?'

'Why do you want to know?' Her voice was sharp. 'You will tell the attendants where I am, won't you? Then they will shut me in my room and I shall never find him!'

'No, it isn't that,' I said, hurriedly. 'It's to help you find your baby. If I know your name, I might be able to find his birth certificate or a record of baptism.'

'So you can read?' She looked rather surprised.

'Of course I can! What sort of school do you think I went to?'

She laughed. 'You are very amusing. Do you mean to be?'

I forced a smile. 'I try.'

'My baby's name is Thomas,' she said. 'After his father. He promised me we would marry. He was the only person who listened to me. He was so . . . affectionate.'

'That's nice,' I said, realising I probably didn't need to ask the older Thomas's surname. 'How did you meet him?'

'He used to sneak upstairs to me when he'd finished his duties. He told me stories about the servants' hall – so much more fun than a ball!' She clapped her hands, beaming. Then her smile faded. 'Or he did until he vanished. When I asked why Thomas was not waiting on us at breakfast as usual, Mama and Papa told me he had received an urgent message from his family and would be gone for some time.' Her brow wrinkled. 'I wonder why he did not say goodbye to me. I had done nothing to anger him.'

Oh dear. The likely scenario was beginning to piece itself together in my mind. 'That's a real shame,' I said. 'Please would you tell me your name? It would definitely help me to find your baby. I promise I won't tell the attendants.' *The attendants*, I thought grimly, *have probably gone where they deserve.*

'Cross your heart and hope to die?' she said. Suddenly, she looked like a little girl telling me a secret.

'Absolutely.' I crossed my heart for good measure.

'Mary Elizabeth Henrietta Sweeney,' she said. 'I was named for my mother and grandmothers.'

'Gosh,' I said. 'I'm Tasha.'

'*Tasha?*' She giggled so hard that she nearly overbalanced. 'What sort of name is that? It sounds like a dog's name.' Her laughter was brought up short as people hurried by. 'Oh no, here they come again!'

'Who are they?' I asked. 'Do you know them?'

'Know *them*? With their rough trousers and common boots? Certainly not. They are looking for something – or someone – but they refuse to help *me*. Just like that woman in the silly frilly gown and the enormous hat. It had an actual bird on it – imagine! She was sending her footmen this way and that, telling them the thief might have dropped her necklace, and when I greeted her she ignored me. How rude! And as for those people with torches…' She drew herself up proudly. 'They do not know who I am, poor things.'

I bet they don't. If they could see you, they'd be over the moon. I glanced at my watch. Ten to one!

'I'm afraid I have to go,' I said, and scrambled to my feet.

'We have not concluded our conversation!' Mary looked most put out. 'We have not discussed the weather, nor enquired about the health of each other's families.'

'We can do that bit next time,' I said. 'I really must go. Good luck in your search.'

I hurried to the entrance, where Nora was waiting with an expectant expression. 'Well?'

'I've got her name and a name for her baby, and she mentioned Napoleon,' I said, 'but she doesn't know why the ghost hunters are here.' I paused. I hated to let Nora down, but I couldn't lie. 'Nora, I'm not sure this is a case. I don't like the sound of what she told me, but I don't think a crime has been committed.'

'Her baby's been taken,' said Nora.

'Yes,' I replied, 'but it's complicated. Nora, I *must* get back. We can talk on the way.'

The return journey to Erskine Street was less convoluted, as Nora was too low in spirit to do more than sidestep the occasional passer-by. She didn't say anything until we were standing outside Erskine Street police station. 'I'll keep trying.' Her head was up, her chin firm.

'I know you will,' I said. 'I'll find out what I can. Please, Nora, go to the Bridewell.'

'I suppose that's an order,' she muttered.

'I'm afraid it is.'

I watched her go, then pushed the glass door. I signed in, using the clock behind the desk this time, returned the coat to lost property, and hurried to the main office.

As soon as I got through the door, I felt Sergeant Doughty glowering at me from his desk. And I hadn't even had lunch.

CHAPTER 6

'Would you care to explain, Constable Saunders, why you have taken over an hour for your lunch?' Sergeant Doughty's voice was dangerously silky. The voice of a film villain who's all charm until he releases the piranhas.

'I, er…'

'On second thoughts, I'm not interested in whatever excuse you plan to give me. And don't tell me that you went on your lunch break late. I've been to the front desk and your signing-out time was a good ten minutes later than the truth.'

'I'm sorry, sir, my watch must be wrong. I'll make sure—'

'And I'm prepared to bet that whatever time you've just written will be similarly incorrect. In your favour.'

'I'm sorry, sir. I was running an errand and I must have lost track of time.'

'Mmm. I thought you were a trustworthy and reliable officer, Constable Saunders.' He rocked slightly on the balls of his feet, letting his displeasure sink in. 'Clearly, however, I was wrong. I wonder how many times you have pulled off this little trick and, as it were, stuck a finger up at the system.'

'Sir, I would never—'

'Laughing at your colleagues who are stupid enough to respect the rules.' His gaze strayed to Steph for a moment. Luckily, she was looking at her screen. She was trying to spare me from any further embarrassment, bless her, but I was already close to sinking into the floor. 'However leaden they may be, however uninspired, they at least do their duty. Unlike you.'

'Sergeant Doughty, I swear this will never happen again.'

His smile could have turned milk. 'I believe you, Constable Saunders. Because I shall be keeping a very close eye on you in future.' He leaned towards me, still wearing that sickening smile, and it was all I could do not to pull back. 'Just think, if I hadn't returned to my desk for some paperwork, I would never have known what you were up to.' He straightened up. 'Frankly, I expected better from you and I am disappointed.' He began to walk to his desk, then wheeled round. 'Oh yes. Since you clearly have time to spare, I've taken the liberty of sending some work your way.'

'Yes, sir,' I muttered.

My in-tray, which before lunch had had a few bits of paper in it, was groaning. Suppressing a rude word, I grabbed the topmost items – I needed both hands – and plonked them on my desk. First up was a document held together with a plastic slide-on spine, like a school project. It looked at least fifty pages thick, and on the front was a post-it note which said *Prepare a two-page summary of the key points* in Sergeant Doughty's spidery hand. When I flicked through it, I discovered that it had been printed double-sided.

I paged through the rest of the pile, which wasn't much better.

'I want those done in order, please, Constable Saunders,' said Sergeant Doughty. 'Starting from the top.'

Across the room, someone sniggered.

'Yes, sir,' I said, and created a new document on the computer with a few savage keystrokes.

I was reading page five and wondering when I would be finished with the darn thing when Inspector Farnsworth appeared in the doorway of his office. Tall and broad, he almost filled it. 'A word, sergeant, if you would.'

Sergeant Doughty stood up. 'Right you are, sir.' He headed for the inspector's office, giving me a beady look on the way.

I leaned back in my chair and closed my eyes. 'Flaming man,' I muttered. 'He would catch me today, of all days.'

'You were pushing your luck,' said Steph. 'What was he supposed to do, give you a medal?'

I goggled at her. 'Whose side are you on?'

'Don't be ridiculous.' She leaned towards me and lowered her voice. 'Even if it was only a few minutes, you were still in the wrong and he'd never let that go.' Her eyes narrowed. 'What were you doing, anyway? Don't tell me the queue at the kebab shop was that long.'

'I wasn't at the kebab shop. I—' Then I thought again. If I told Steph what I'd really been doing, she'd probably be furious that I'd gone off on a mission without her. Not that she'd have come. In any case, it wasn't a conversation I was prepared to have in the middle of the office. 'I was picking up some bits for Mum and it took longer than I thought.'

Steph looked round me. 'I don't see any bags.'

'Didn't need one: it's sewing stuff. Embroidery silks, that sort of thing.'

'Right.' Steph didn't seem remotely convinced. 'If you'd told Sergeant Doughty that, he'd probably have let you off. He lets you get away with murder most of the time anyway.'

'He does not.'

'Then why do I get saddled with the crap, eh?' She glared at the pile of paper on my desk. 'What you've got there is exactly the kind of soul-destroying admin I usually end up with.' Her lip curled. 'Welcome to my world, Tasha.'

Feeling the world was plain unfair – though I did see Steph's point about her never-decreasing paperwork – I turned to the report just as Sergeant Doughty re-entered the main office. He paused by my desk. 'I hope we weren't chatting instead of working, Constable.'

'I'm hard at work, sir,' I said, gazing at the report as if my life depended on it. I had the feeling that if I met the sergeant's eyes, I would turn him to stone. Then again, that would be an end to my problems.

Even as I realised that, he strolled towards his corner, completely unharmed. 'I want that summary on my desk by close of play, Constable Saunders, and you'll stay until it's done.'

'Yes, sir,' I muttered.

The afternoon wore on. Then, oh blessed respite, Sergeant Doughty, who had been issuing curt monosyllables down his phone for the last two minutes, stood up. 'Constable Sharpe!'

'Yes, sir?' Steph was doing her best not to look worried.

'Punch-up outside St John's shopping centre. Several witnesses to take statements from. Get moving.'

'Yes, sir.' Steph didn't need telling twice. Her notebook was in her pocket and her hat on within ten seconds.

'Bye,' I muttered, as she hurried after the sergeant.

He paused in the doorway. 'Constable Saunders, if I hear from anyone that you've left your desk for more than two minutes while I'm gone, you'll be for the high jump. Do I make myself clear?'

'As crystal, sir,' I said, and turned another page. *I might as well be in detention.*

The hands of the clock crawled round. At one point, I thought they were going backwards. At least I was halfway through the report and had some bullet points. Three pages of bullet points, but at least I had something.

Then I had a bright idea. Sergeant Doughty clearly wasn't easing off any time soon – but what if I appealed to a higher authority? Inspector Farnsworth was in, and my lunchtime encounter was right up his street. Maybe I could kill two birds with one stone: get the inspector's help, and ask him to lift my punishment.

I got up, walked to the inspector's office, and knocked on the door.

'Yes?' said a weary voice.

I put my head round the door. 'It's me, sir. Is now a bad time?'

'Define a good time,' he said, his face deadpan.

'Er… Would you mind if I sat down?'

He sighed. 'I don't suppose I can stop you, Constable Saunders.' That was the other thing about spending less time at the Bridewell. In Erskine Street, it was all Constable Saunders this, Constable Saunders that from the inspector – when I saw him – and never Tasha.

'I'm in a bit of hot water,' I began. I looked round to check the door was closed properly. 'It's because of Nora.'

'Mm. I was unable to avoid hearing what the good sergeant said earlier. So you effectively falsified your timesheet.'

That I hadn't expected. 'It was only a few minutes, sir. I was in early. Nora—'

'Nora is a ghost,' said Inspector Farnsworth. His tone suggested his patience was wearing thin.

'She might have a new case. A woman's searching for her baby, and there are ghost hunters around, so something must be up, and—'

The inspector held up a hand. 'Let me stop you there. I can tell you're very invested in this, Constable Saunders, and it certainly sounds much more interesting than whatever Sergeant Doughty has given you to do, but I cannot condone your actions today. To do so would set a dangerous precedent, particularly as we are currently in a position where we must show the utmost integrity at all times.'

My heart sank. 'Yes, sir.'

'So no, I won't let you skip your duties and go off on a wild-ghost chase.' For a moment he looked pleased with himself, in rather the sort of way that Sergeant Doughty often did. 'We have more work at the moment than we can possibly manage—'

'Which is why I shouldn't be summarising documents.'

The inspector regarded me coolly. 'Did you interrupt me, Constable Saunders?'

I knew I was beaten. 'No, Inspector Farnsworth.' I couldn't bring myself to call him sir, not just then.

'I thought not. I suggest you return to your desk and get on with your work. Especially if you wish to leave at a reasonable hour tonight.' He bent his head to the document he was reading.

'I'm sorry, sir.'

Silence.

'I'll see myself out.'

I slunk to my desk and stared at the report. After a few minutes, having taken in nothing, I turned the page. I felt small, the smallest I ever had in the police force, even less significant than a new recruit. No one was on my side – and there was nothing I could do about it.

CHAPTER 7

Steph returned to the office at half past four, looking full of purpose. 'Hi,' she said, pausing by my desk.

'Hello. I take it you had fun?'

'I wouldn't call it fun,' said Steph, with a slight frown. 'I've been working.'

'But you enjoyed it.'

'It was satisfying. No one saw the whole thing, but we could piece together what happened from the various accounts. We've got some good descriptions. Sergeant Doughty will get a facial composite done.'

'Jolly good.'

An awkward silence fell. 'Are you still working on that report?' Steph said, after a while.

'I am.'

'I'll make you a drink. Tea?'

'Coffee, please. Strong.'

A few minutes later, she put the Snoopy mug on my desk. Steam was coming out of his head. 'I washed your mug for you.'

'Thank you.'

'I'll let you get on.' She went to her desk, switched on the computer and sat down. She was practically bristling with efficiency. Then she looked over. 'We could do something together after work. Go and see a film, maybe.'

'Maybe,' I replied. *She's even efficient when she's asking me out.* 'I might have to stay late to get this done.'

'Oh. OK.' She turned to her screen. 'Better get these notes typed up, I guess.' A couple of minutes later she was in a world of her own, tapping away at her keyboard.

Typical, I thought. *The one day I plan to stay in the office, for my own perfectly good reasons, you want to go out. Normally I can't drag you out of here.*

Once my initial surprise had worn off, Inspector Farnsworth's lack of interest in the case had spurred me on. If I was the only person who cared, fine. I'd investigate solo. I felt slightly guilty that I hadn't involved Steph, but it was too late to go back on that now – and it would involve admitting that I'd fibbed earlier. I'd already had quite enough drama for one day, thank you very much.

In reality, the report summary I'd been tasked with was almost done. My plan was to wait until everyone had headed off, then do a bit of research. Not on the office computer – I wasn't that daft – but using an incognito browser on my phone. If I couldn't get any useful information from Mary, maybe I could find out what the ghost hunters were so interested in.

The minute hand of the clock crept towards the hour. At two minutes to, Sergeant Doughty stood up. 'Right, you lot, I've got to be somewhere in fifteen minutes so I'm leaving on the dot. Anyone got work that can't wait till tomorrow?' He glanced at me. 'That doesn't include you, Constable Saunders.'

The rest of the office joined in a ragged chorus of 'No, boss' and 'No, sir.'

'Get yourselves packed up, then. A good day's work. We've made some interesting discoveries.' He gave me a significant look. Normally I'd have worried about being in the sergeant's bad books, but right now I just wanted him to get lost and take the team with him.

Steph clicked her mouse a few times and her computer powered down. 'I hope you don't have to stay too late,' she said. 'Text me when you're nearly done.'

'Sure.' I felt twitchy, and I willed myself to keep looking at the report while she packed her bag.

'See you later.' She smiled and strolled out. *I bet she's forgotten what finishing on time feels like.*

The others trailed out, and Sergeant Doughty came out of the inspector's office. 'On my desk before you leave, Constable,' he said, and walked out whistling.

The sounds of chatter and closing doors faded until all that was left was the ticking of the clock. The inspector's door was shut.

The first thing I did was fish the emergency Snickers bar from my bag. Then I opened an incognito browser window on my phone and typed *ghost St George's Hall Liverpool* in the search box.

I wasn't prepared for the flood of results which followed. I amended my search to include the year and clicked the search button.

This time, the first result was *Spooky goings-on at St George's Hall.* The link took me to a week-old article from the local newspaper.

A group on a guided tour at St George's Hall got more than they bargained for when they heard eerie noises in the Great Hall, I read.

The group, who had come from North Wales for a mini break in the city, reported hearing scraping noises coming from the hall's ceiling. 'At first I thought it was workmen because of the scaffolding,' said Eileen Hawkins, 62. 'When I looked up, no one was there.'

'It was peculiar,' said her husband Geoff, 66. 'A sort of scrabbling. It sent a shiver down my spine, I can tell you.'

However, the tour guide, Sue Marsden, wasn't fazed by the interruption. 'Old buildings make noises *all the time,' she said. 'The ceiling renovation in the Great Hall begins soon. I expect it's something to do with that. I moved the group along swiftly and we heard no more unexpected noises.'*

The ceiling renovation is expected to take some time, since it requires an expert restoration team, but the Great Hall will remain open to tours with minor access restrictions. Please see the St George's Hall website for details.

I closed the article, frowning. Surely a bit of scraping and scrabbling wasn't enough to bring an army of ghost hunters to the hall and its surroundings. Then again, I'd watched ghost-hunting programmes on TV. In my view, they got way too excited about the smallest things, making a mountain out of practically nothing. And the timing, I had to admit, was perfect. I made a note of the names on my phone, in case I wanted to follow up with any of them, and scrolled down the search results. *Ghost story event at Liverpool Central Library . . . Showing times for Ghostbusters at Liverpool Odeon . . . Ghost clothing, stockists in Liverpool...* Nothing else seemed to fit.

I finished the Snickers bar, then typed my name and the date at the bottom of my summary, printed it out, and put it in the middle of Sergeant Doughty's desk. 'I'm heading off, sir,' I called, in the direction of Inspector Farnsworth's door, and unlocked my phone to text Steph.

Then I paused. What if I returned to St John's Gardens? I could chat to a couple of ghost hunters and find out what they were looking for. I might be able to get more information from Mary. If the hall was still open, maybe I could talk to a tour guide.

I stuffed my phone in my bag and switched off the computer. I'd be, what, an hour? That would mean I'd be back at Steph's by six thirty at latest. More than enough time to go out. Hopefully, I'd have new findings to celebrate.

Lost property was shut, but luckily the undercover coat was still hanging on the rack: a baggy navy duffel which was meant to hide uniform when needed, but was mostly used as an emergency raincoat. I slipped it on and buttoned it over my uniform, then left, making sure to sign out using the time on the wall clock.

Two minutes after leaving the station, it started pouring. 'For heaven's sake,' I muttered, putting up my hood. At least I had the coat.

I stomped along, ducking and weaving through a sea of people who seemed determined to bump into me and poke me with their umbrellas. *It's as if the world's against me.* I plodded on bravely, attempting to avoid the fast-forming puddles.

The journey took even longer than it had with Nora at lunchtime, as the streets were crowded with people trying to get home, or into a pub. Cars shot past me as if they'd shrink in the rain. Finally, though, I scurried down William Brown Street and into St John's Gardens.

And of course, it was deserted. Apart from the statues – and if they could have climbed off their pedestals and nipped into the World Museum for a cuppa, I reckon they would have.

'Fair-weather ghost hunters,' I muttered, kicking a loose pebble. I did a hasty circuit, in case I'd missed something, but my only companions were the rain and the combined smells of damp vegetation and damp wool.

Mary, presumably, was sheltering somewhere. Could she be in St George's Hall? I hurried out of the Queen Square exit and turned left, but the metal doors of the hall, which seemed small though they were at least twice my height, were closed. 'Don't they know people work nine to five?' I muttered.

Could she be on St George's Plateau? I climbed the steps, shining with rain, and peered through the haze, but there was no sign of Mary. She wasn't snuggling up to a lion, leaning on a pillar, or sheltering under the horses of Victoria or Albert. She was nowhere.

Well, that was pointless. I sighed and headed for Steph's flat, my boots squelching in the rain. When I was ten minutes away, I texted. *All done, heading out now. See you soon X.* Then I pocketed the phone and carried on walking.

I reached Steph's apartment block, one of several

which had sprung up out of nowhere in the last few years, and rang the bell. Steph took a couple of minutes to answer. 'Come up,' she said, and the door buzzed.

That's not much of a welcome, I thought, as I walked upstairs. I generally took the stairs, as Steph's flat was only on the second floor and the lift was out of action more often than not. *She's probably found more work to do and now she wants to stay in.*

When I got to Steph's flat the door was closed, which was unusual: she normally left it open for me. I knocked, and it opened almost immediately.

Steph was frowning, and she was wearing tracksuit bottoms and a sweatshirt. Not anything she'd go out in. 'Where have you been?'

'At the station.'

'Don't lie. I rang your work number half an hour ago and you weren't there.'

'I was probably making a brew.'

'No you weren't!' she fired back, immediately. 'Inspector Farnsworth answered and he said you left at quarter past five. So where were you?'

I stared at her, completely wrong-footed.

'Just tell me. And no more lies. No matter what it is, I want the truth.'

CHAPTER 8

I honestly didn't know where to start. 'Um, this probably looks bad, but—'

'Yes. It does.' For a small person, Steph did a remarkably good job of filling the doorway.

'Could I come in?' I asked. 'I'd rather not have this conversation on the landing…' I realised how that sounded, and fell silent.

'Maybe you shouldn't have lied to me, then. It's been quite a day for it, hasn't it? What with fiddling your timesheet earlier, and now this.' Her nose wrinkled. 'This had better be good.'

'It isn't as bad as you think, Steph—'

'You have no idea what I think!' Steph and I stared at each other, but she was blinking rapidly, as if to keep back tears. 'So, are you?'

'Am I what?'

'You're going to make me say it, are you? Fine. Are you seeing someone else?'

I goggled at her. 'No, of course not! Why would you think that?'

'Er, today's events? The fact that you always want to go out after work and I never have the energy?' She ran her hand through her short hair. 'It's not that I don't want to, but I have to pull my weight – more than my weight, if Sergeant Doughty has anything to do with it – or I'll get sent back to Cheshire Police. To a station where the big case last year was someone pinching people's hubcaps.' A tear trickled down her cheek and she scrubbed it out with her hand. 'Oh, for God's sake.'

I rushed forward and wrapped her in my arms, and she shook with tears. I steered her into the flat and closed the door behind us.

'Sorry,' she choked out.

'No, *I'm* sorry.' And I was. I had never thought of how Steph might see my silly sneaking around. I stroked her hair. 'I should have told you straightaway, but it was never the right time, or you were busy, or someone was nearby—'

Her head jerked up and she stared at me.

'It's Nora,' I said. 'She turned up in the kitchen this morning with a mission.'

The fear in Steph's eyes melted into confusion. 'But you weren't at the Bridewell today. It's Thursday.'

'Exactly. When I went to the kitchen to make you a

brew – remember? – Nora was there. She's cooked up a way to get the superintendent to send her places.'

Steph took my hand and pulled me towards the sofa, then flopped down, taking me with her. 'So they're mobile.'

'Nora is. Providing a police officer orders her to be. She can't order the superintendent, though, so I guess he's stuck.'

'That might not be such a bad thing,' Steph murmured. Then her brow furrowed. 'Wait a minute. So what's this mission?'

'She saw a ghost, in a sort of dream.'

Steph regarded me in silence for a good few seconds. I saw her weigh up my words, and felt terrible. What if Steph couldn't trust me any more? I didn't know what I would do. Then, at last, she sighed. 'Go on.'

I told Steph about Nora's recurring visions, her trip to St John's Gardens, my lunchtime visit there, Mary Sweeney's story and the strange goings-on at St George's Hall. 'Here's the article I found,' I said, showing her it on my phone. 'That's where I went after work, to talk to some ghost hunters, but they'd gone home because of the rain.'

Steph laughed. 'Serves you right for leaving me out of it. If it was up to me, you'd have gone without a coat and got soaked through.'

'Close enough.' I shrugged off the soggy coat and

put my hand on hers. 'I'm really sorry, Steph. Nora asked me to help and I admit it, I was flattered. An investigation of my own. I got carried away, and I should have known better.'

'Well, you've had your punishment,' said Steph. 'You're definitely on Sergeant Doughty's radar now. I thought I was the only person he looked at like that.'

I shrugged. 'Maybe the heat's off you, then.'

'That'll make a nice change,' Steph replied. She squeezed my hand. 'Sorry. I assumed the worst and I should have trusted you.' She stared into the middle distance. 'I can't believe Nora's at large.'

'As far as the superintendent will let her be,' I said.

'I guess. He won't want Nora to have too much of the glory.' She grinned.

'I'm so sorry that I made you think the worst,' I said. 'I never considered how it would look. I never thought you'd think I would cheat on you.'

'Why not?' said Steph. 'From time to time, I wonder how I ever got you to go out with me in the first place. I've been a rubbish partner lately. Frankly, I wouldn't date me.'

'Don't be daft,' I murmured, and reached for her.

***

Some time later, I brought Steph a cup of tea in bed. I figured it was the least I could do.

'Thanks,' she said. 'You're not going to tell me that Nora's in my kitchen, are you?'

'What a thought.' I giggled. 'Knowing Nora, if she was here she'd probably pop into the bedroom for a chat.'

Steph pulled the bedclothes up to her neck. 'Don't even joke about it.'

I passed Steph her dressing gown, just in case, and got into bed. 'Seriously, though, what will we do? Sergeant Doughty's got his beady eye on me and the inspector won't help.' I filled Steph in on the deeply unsatisfying conversation I'd had with him.

'That's weird,' said Steph. 'It's exactly the sort of thing he'd like. Delving into history and digging in records.'

I spread my hands. 'But right now, he isn't biting.'

'OK.' Steph pondered. 'So your work wings have been clipped, it's unlikely the sergeant will ease up on me, Huw's not back till Monday week, and we can meet Nora for an hour at the Bridewell every other day. Assuming she's there, that is.'

'Thanks for the optimistic view,' I said, grimacing.

'Any time.' Steph sipped her tea. 'There's only one thing for it.' She put the mug on her bedside table.

'What's that, superbrain?'

'We'll have to investigate in our own time. Luckily, I have just the thing to help us. Wait there.' She got up, pulled on her dressing gown, then rooted in her work bag.

'What are you looking for? A crystal ball? A time

machine?'

'Better than that,' said Steph. 'Well, maybe.' She held up a key ring with three keys on it: one large, the others slightly smaller.

I frowned at them. 'Unless one of those is the magic key from the Biff, Chip and Kipper books, I don't see how—' Then it clicked. 'They're the keys to the Bridewell.'

'Yup.' Steph threw the keys up and watched them spin and jingle until they dropped into her palm. 'Front door, yard door, file room. I got spares cut not long after we wrapped up the Four Fingers case. The keys to the Bridewell went missing for days once. The inspector and I searched high and low for them. We found them at the back of Huw's top drawer: he'd borrowed them and completely forgotten about them. I decided we needed an insurance policy.'

I stared at her with new respect. 'Stephanie Sharpe, I never knew you could be so sneaky.'

'I got it from you,' she said, grinning. 'And possibly Nora. Speaking of which, shall we grab a bite to eat, then head to the Bridewell? I figure we have news to share with our two colleagues on the case.'

I smacked my forehead. 'I knew I'd forgotten something – Mum's lasagne is still in the fridge at work!'

Steph nudged me with her elbow. 'In that case,

shall we eat out?'

I beamed at her. 'It's a date.'

***

The Bridewell was eerie at night, looming over us like an angry giant. I found myself swallowing nervously as Steph worked the key in the lock. Eventually, the door swung open with an ominous creak.

'Nora!' called Steph. 'Superintendent Hicks!' She snapped on the lights. It was still creepy.

Silence.

'It's Steph and Tasha. We want to talk to you about the St John's Gardens case.'

We waited. The harsh lights overhead cast sharp shadows, and I tried not to think of what might be lurking in them.

'They could be in the yard,' I said, to distract myself. 'Or the file room, or—'

'What are you doing here at this time?' said Nora's voice, from above. She was peeping through the wrought-iron banisters at us. 'And what on earth are you wearing?'

'Plain clothes,' I replied. 'We aren't officially here.'

'Well, I can see you.' Nora turned. 'It's all right, Superintendent, it really is them. You'll have to ignore their silly outfits.'

'Excuse me,' I said. 'These boots were in *Grazia* last month.'

Nora sniggered. 'Maybe they should have stayed there. You look as if you're going to take Queen Vic out for a gallop.'

Superintendent Hicks stuck his head over the banister. 'Good heavens,' he said, taking us in. 'To what do we owe the pleasure, ladies?'

Steph smiled. 'We've come to investigate. Let's head to the detective office and get cracking.'

***

'It still seems odd to me,' said Nora, once we'd given her chapter and verse on the latest developments. 'Is whatever's making the noises in St George's Hall anything to do with poor Mary Sweeney? If it *is* a ghost, what is it trying to do? Is it trying to attract people's attention, or distract them from something?'

'These are good questions, Sergeant Norris,' said the superintendent. Nora wasn't really a sergeant – when I'd asked Steph, she told me that Inspector Farnsworth had referred to Nora as Sergeant Norris on the Athenaeum case to butter up a snobbish ghost – but as far as the superintendent was concerned, the promotion was permanent. He nodded wisely. 'In my view, there is an obvious way to find out the answers.'

Steph and I looked at each other. 'I'm afraid your reasoning is too sophisticated for mere constables, Superintendent,' said Steph. 'Would you mind explaining?'

The superintendent stretched his legs out under the desk. 'Of course. This ghost doesn't seem inclined to go out and meet the ghost hunters, or you would know about it from that spider's web that you're always surfing. If my terminology is correct.'

I hid a smile. 'Spot on, Superintendent.'

'So if the ghost won't come to you, you must go to the ghost. You know there are guided tours of St George's Hall, because of the newspaper article. So book yourselves on one, and perhaps all will be revealed.'

'You can go undercover in your funny clothes!' said Nora, beaming.

'Normal clothes, Nora,' said Steph, with an eye-roll. 'Now that you've left the Bridewell a few times, you know what people are wearing these days.'

'That doesn't mean they aren't funny,' said Nora. 'Anyway, will you do it?'

I raised my eyebrows at Steph. 'Do we have a choice?'

'I guess not,' said Steph. But she was smiling too.

CHAPTER 9

Steph and I had laid the ground carefully. Sergeant Doughty would never give the pair of us the same day off. He would cite business need and manpower – ugh – and probably end by refusing leave to both of us. So Steph asked him if she could take Monday off, on the grounds that she had leave which had to be used before the end of March.

Meanwhile, I seized a rare moment when Sergeant Doughty was out of the office and Inspector Farnsworth was in, and asked him. 'My auntie's visiting from Australia,' I said, 'and she wants to do the tour of St George's Hall. It might be good for me to learn a bit of history, too. About the courts, and the assizes, and everything.'

The inspector gave me a long look. 'Does this have anything to do with Nora?'

'There's that, too,' I said. 'At least I'm doing it in my own time and showing my auntie round the city.

Isn't that a better approach?'

Inspector Farnsworth sighed. 'I suppose so. All right, leave authorised. I'll put it in the calendar.'

'Thank you, sir.' I resisted the urge to punch the air as I left his office.

Of course, one of us could have gone and reported back to the other, but it wouldn't have been the same. And having already got myself in trouble by keeping secrets, I wanted to be as open with Steph as possible from now on.

So we booked ourselves on the eleven am tour and on Monday morning, in our civvies, let ourselves into the Bridewell.

'I don't see why you need both of us,' grumbled Superintendent Hicks. 'The pair of you plus Nora is more than enough.'

'Some people are never happy,' I said. 'If we'd proposed to take just Nora, you'd have complained about being left out. We thought you'd appreciate a trip. Besides, four pairs of eyes are better than three. Or two, or one.'

'Yes, you've made your point,' said the superintendent. 'But if something happens to the Bridewell when none of us are here to guard it, don't go blaming me.'

'We won't. Let's go.'

The superintendent goggled when we went outside. 'Where's the car?'

'It's a fifteen-minute walk, Superintendent,' said Steph. 'We're on leave, so we can't borrow a police car, can we?'

The superintendent reached for his pipe. Throughout the journey, he comforted himself by puffing out clouds of ghostly smoke and muttering. I occasionally caught a few words, such as 'most irregular', or 'wouldn't have happened in my day.'

We reached the hall in plenty of time, so I suggested a turn in the gardens, hoping to encounter either Mary or the ghost hunters who had been conspicuous by their absence on my last visit. However, the few people wandering aimlessly along the paths seemed to be there purely to take the air. 'Typical,' I murmured. 'A nice day and not a ghost about.'

'I wouldn't say that,' said the superintendent, 'but they're very faint. Mostly in uniform…' Suddenly he waved an arm as if flagging a taxi. 'Hey, you!'

I followed the superintendent's gaze and saw a navy blur move rapidly away.

'French soldier, I reckon,' said the superintendent. 'Doubt he'd be much use.'

'Can you see them?' I asked Nora.

'Not a sausage,' she replied cheerfully.

I checked my watch. 'Come on, let's go in. Maybe we can chat to the staff before we do the tour.'

Steph nudged me. 'Don't be too full on, Tasha,'

she said.

'Me, full on?' I said, eyes wide. 'You must be thinking of someone else.'

'That's exactly what I mean,' said Steph.

We entered and approached the reception desk. 'Hi,' said Steph. 'We're here for the tour.'

'Oh yes,' said the woman behind the desk. She looked hard at us, then at a document she pulled from a drawer. 'Just the two of you?'

I was about to correct her when Steph said 'Yes, that's right.' *OK, fair point.* I resolved to speak only when spoken to.

'Right, if you'll take a seat.' She motioned to a bench where three or four people were already sitting. *Hmmm*, I thought, noting their puffer jackets. Then panic seized me – what if one of them saw Nora and the superintendent and raised the alarm? But none of them seemed remotely interested in us: they were too busy chatting.

Superintendent Hicks strode past me and took one of the vacant spaces on the bench. My eyes widened with indignation, but of course I couldn't say anything. 'You sit: I don't mind standing,' I said to Steph.

'That'd look weird,' she said, out of the side of her mouth.

Another couple in puffer jackets came up to the desk. 'Two for the tour, please,' said the male half, slapping a twenty-pound note on the counter.

The woman opened the drawer again and consulted the document. 'Sorry, no can do,' she replied. 'No known ghost hunters, by order of the management.'

'That's ridiculous!' cried the female half of the couple.

The woman behind the desk slammed her drawer shut. 'According to our records, you've disrupted at least three tours with your relentless questioning of the guide. Therefore, you are banned. Please leave before I call security.'

'Ridiculous,' muttered the man as they stalked off. 'Call this a free country?' was his parting shot, delivered over his shoulder.

The puffer jackets on the bench were exchanging worried glances. One, a young woman with a blonde ponytail and a resolute air, murmured 'One question each, *maximum.*'

A capable-looking thirty-something woman with a dark bob walked up. She was dressed in a knee-length dark skirt and a white blouse. 'Good morning,' she said. 'My name is Sue and I'll be your tour guide today. We'll visit the cells, the court, the Great Hall and the concert room.' I was itching to ask if she was Sue Marsden from the article, but mindful of my resolution to keep my gob shut, I checked her badge instead. *Su Hope*, it said. 'I'll take you through the housekeeping and then we'll get going.' We fidgeted while she outlined the procedure in case of fire and asked about access issues. 'Right, off we go.'

It was a fascinating tour. As Su talked, I found myself visualising the carriage drawing up, packed with people on remand, and following them on their journey. I could almost smell the stench of the packed cells, and hear the hubbub in the court as the accused trembled in the dock and the public who'd come for a grand day out sized them up.

'Anyone know why the dock is so big?' asked Su, indicating the generous space.

Heads were shaken.

'Gangs,' she said. 'Sometimes the police made multiple arrests, especially when the gangs were at their height in the second half of the nineteenth century, and they had to be able to fit them all in.'

I imagined several villainous men crowded together, and wondered whether the people sitting near them had been scared.

'Were any notable criminals tried here?' asked the woman with the blonde ponytail. She sneaked a little notebook from her pocket.

'Too many to name,' said Su, with a smile. I could tell she'd had that question before. 'If you go online, you'll find plenty of information. The British Newspaper Archive will have reports of trials, or you could check the Liverpool Record Office archives at Central Library.'

'Thank you,' said Blonde Ponytail, and made a surreptitious note.

We suffered through an account of the building's air conditioning, and several members of the group were drooping, but when Su said 'Let's move on to the Great Hall,' everyone perked up. Several people hung back, whispering.

She wouldn't let us go in until she'd given us yet more information. When she finally opened the door, we gasped.

It was magnificent. I'd looked at pictures online beforehand, but they hadn't conveyed the scale or the grandeur. The barrel ceiling curved above a vast room, making me feel ant-sized. The chandeliers suspended on each side of the room seemed small in comparison with the great pillars and the arches they supported.

Su talked about the Minton floor, which was protected by a wooden covering. I'm sure it was riveting, but my eye was drawn to the scaffolding rig on the other side of the hall, extending right up to the ceiling and partially hidden by plastic sheeting. I waited for a gap in the narrative, then asked, 'Is that the section of roof that's being restored?'

Su barely glanced at it. 'Yes, work should commence in the next fortnight or so.'

'I thought it had already started.'

Her eyebrows drew together slightly. 'No, there's

been a slight delay. Anyway, to continue what I was saying. As you can see, there are several statues in the Great Hall. We'll begin with William Gladstone…' She made a beeline for one of the statues, and I wondered what it was about William Gladstone that meant he had two statues, one inside, one out.

Steph and I, plus our two companions, formed the tail end of the procession approaching the statue. 'She's got her eye on you now,' said Steph. 'Keep quiet for a bit, and let me do the talking.'

'Uh huh.' I moved towards Nora. 'Can you climb that scaffolding?' I muttered.

Nora gawked at me. 'Me, climb that?'

'Well, I can't, can I?'

Nora sized it up. 'I can try.' She set off, getting smaller and smaller. She was toy-sized by the time she reached it. She stretched for the first horizontal pole but couldn't quite reach.

'Any chance you could boost her up?' I whispered to the superintendent.

He looked outraged. 'Firstly, that is in no way within my duty as a senior police officer. Secondly, I am not laying hands on a fellow officer, *especially* not a female one. Finally, in case you've forgotten, Sergeant Norris and I are both ghosts.'

He folded his arms and we watched Nora stretch in vain. Then she crouched and jumped. Her hands passed through the bar and she returned to the ground. 'Darn,' she said.

'I don't suppose you can see any ghosts in here?' I asked the superintendent.

'Not one,' he said. 'That doesn't mean there aren't any. But I don't sense any, either.'

'Oh well. Let's catch up with the tour. Hopefully the others will ask good questions.'

Nora returned, flapping her hands as if her palms were chafed. We learned from Su how much it had all cost, followed by a detailed account of the huge pipe organ at one end of the room. The puffer-jacketed group were practically twitching with impatience. Finally, it was too much for one of them, a chubby man with thinning brown hair, wearing an orange jacket. 'Have there been any more funny noises in here?' he asked.

The release of tension rippled through the group.

'There weren't any funny noises,' said Su.

'Yes, there were,' said a woman with an intricate French plait. 'It said in the newspaper.'

'Oh, the newspapers will print anything.'

'So why is the work on the ceiling delayed?' The words were out of my mouth before I realised. Steph shot me an accusing glare and I shrugged. 'I'm just asking.'

Su gave me a steely look. 'Are you a ghost hunter?'

I drew myself up. 'No, I'm not.'

'I'm glad to hear it,' she replied, drily. 'In that

case, you won't mind if I take your name, will you? We've had all sorts of trouble from ghost hunters and so-called journalists hijacking our tours.'

'If you must know, I'm a police officer.' I pulled out my warrant card and showed it to her. 'Off duty, obviously. So you can't blame me for having an enquiring mind.'

She looked at the card, then me, then the card again. 'Natasha Saunders, Merseyside Police,' she said. 'I'll remember that name.'

'I don't mind if you do,' I said, then winced as Steph dug me in the ribs.

The rest of the tour passed without incident or further questions. The Great Hall was lovely, as was the concert room with its stunning chandelier, but I'd lost my appetite for history. By the time we made it back to the foyer, I felt as if I'd been tramping round the building for days. *What a waste of a day off,* I thought bitterly. And Inspector Farnsworth's comment about a wild-ghost chase echoed in my head.

CHAPTER 10

We returned to St John's Gardens, which was still quiet, and found a bench. 'What do you think?' Steph asked.

Superintendent Hicks pondered. 'My opinion is that we should repair to a tearoom and consider the matter. It's far too cold to be hanging around in a park.'

I frowned. 'You don't feel the cold.'

'I'm thinking of you two,' said the superintendent. 'You're hiding it well, but I'm sure you're chilly. I'd suggest something a bit stronger to warm you up, but I'm not sure that's a suitable suggestion for a mostly female group.'

'Do they still have Lyons Corner Houses?' asked Nora. 'I used to love those: the waitresses in their little uniforms. I sometimes wondered whether I should have gone for a job there, but my crimefighting impulses were too strong.'

'Weren't you a matron originally?' said Steph.

Nora looked offended. 'If it hadn't been for the Spanish flu – and sexual discrimination, of course – I bet I'd have made a good police officer.' I noted that she avoided meeting the superintendent's eye.

'I'm sure you would,' I said, in an attempt to smooth things over. 'Unfortunately, there aren't any – what was it you said?'

'Lyons Corner Houses,' said Nora, dejectedly.

'There aren't any of those nowadays.'

'I believe they turned into Wimpy bars,' said Superintendent Hicks.

'Can we go to one of those, then?' To give Nora due credit, she was certainly a sticker.

'Sorry, Nora,' said Steph. 'It's not that I don't want to take you, but firstly, we can't discuss an ongoing case in public, and secondly, how would it look for the pair of us to be seen talking to invisible people?'

'I suppose,' Nora admitted grudgingly. Then she brightened. 'Maybe you could take us when it's quiet one day. You wouldn't have to talk to us: we could sit and enjoy the atmosphere.'

'Maybe,' said Steph. She reminded me of a mum saying *We'll see* to her kids. She checked her watch. 'For now, we can head back to the Bridewell. By the time we get there, the coast should be clear.'

We didn't talk much as we strolled up Islington, for which I was grateful. I wasn't sure how I felt about the whole tour experience. It had been enjoyable, certainly, but we had more questions than answers, and more lines of enquiry had opened up for us to investigate. And we were no closer to finding Mary's baby.

As we approached the disused police station, Steph produced her key ring and fitted the large key in the lock.

'We'll go this way,' said Superintendent Hicks. 'I could do with a smoke.' He stepped through the gate into the courtyard. 'Come along, Sergeant Norris.'

'It would be nice to use the door like a civilised person,' said Nora, but she followed the superintendent and walked over to the police horses grazing on ghost grass in the corner.

'What's your take on it all?' I asked Steph quietly as we stepped into the Bridewell.

'Not sure,' said Steph. 'Too many possibilities, not enough information.'

'That's exactly how I feel,' I said. 'Think of all the ghosts who could be haunting St George's Hall. I bet some of them died in those cells. At least there weren't any hangings.'

'Oh don't,' said Steph. 'And we know from the ghosts we've met that they don't necessarily haunt the place where they died. Who's to say that there aren't hundreds of ghosts lurking in St George's Hall who don't believe they had a fair trial?'

'Plus that French soldier the superintendent saw in the gardens,' I added. 'What was he doing there? Was he on trial, or was it something to do with the cemetery?'

'Oh heck, I'd forgotten the cemetery,' said Steph. 'This is a nightmare.'

'Don't take this the wrong way, but I'm glad it's not just me who thinks that.' I gave her a one-armed hug. 'Shall we make a brew?'

Steph considered. 'Best not. I mean, I doubt anyone's monitoring electricity usage, but someone might notice their milk's gone down – that's if there is any. We can't afford to alert anyone to our presence here. It doesn't feel like trespassing, but I suppose it is.'

'It's rather exciting, isn't it?' I drew closer to her. 'Here out of hours, all alone…'

'There you are!' cried Nora, from the end of the corridor. 'We thought you'd be in the detective office.'

'We were about to go up,' I said, having beat a speedy retreat as soon as I heard Nora's voice. 'We thought we should wait for you two to finish whatever you were doing.'

'Maybe I should have done that, too,' said Nora, and winked at me. She turned. 'It's all right, Superintendent, you're safe to enter.'

Upstairs, Steph pulled a couple of folded sheets of paper from her bag and spread them on the desk, then dug around for a pen. 'Normally we'd have an investigation board,' she said, 'but obviously that won't do here.'

'What a shame,' said Nora, pouting.

'We'll have to make do.' Steph wrote *KNOWLEDGE SO FAR* at the top of the first sheet. 'What do we know?'

'Not enough,' said Superintendent Hicks.

'I agree, but what do we know for sure?'

'People heard scraping noises,' I said. 'Or they thought they did, and the tour guide tried to play it down by blaming the building.'

'Tasha and I saw the ghost from my vision in St John's Gardens,' said Nora. 'Her name is Mary Sweeney, she's searching for her baby, and she told us her parents sent her there. She didn't think she was in the hospital. She said she was shut in a room. She's being disturbed by the ghost hunters.'

'Could she have anything to do with the noises in the Great Hall?' asked Steph, as she scribbled.

Nora and I both shrugged. 'Why would she be scraping at the ceiling?' said Nora. 'She won't find her baby in there. Whenever I've seen her, she's been wandering in the gardens.'

'I saw a ghost in uniform,' said Superintendent Hicks. 'And there was a court here, and a hospital, and a cemetery, and who knows what else.'

'We can look that up,' I said, and Steph wrote

Research previous buildings.

'Didn't the tour guide mention records in Central Library?' said Nora.

'Yes, and online.' Steph made another note. 'I can take those. Have you got a library card, Tasha?'

'No, but I could get one.'

'I wonder if the Athenaeum has any information in its ghost books,' said Superintendent Hicks. 'I could ask Mr Chapman the librarian to check for me.'

'Oh, that's a good idea,' said Nora, and the superintendent shot her a pleased look.

'Why didn't we see Mary today?' I said. 'I'd have thought she'd be around, what with the ghost hunters coming on the tour.'

'Have you had any more visions, Nora?' asked the superintendent.

'I haven't, sir, not since you made me go to Erskine Street.'

'Does that mean we can put her aside and concentrate on the other ghost?' asked Steph.

'No!' Nora and I said, together. 'We have to help her find her baby,' I added. 'Well, find out about her baby, then judge whether we should tell her.'

'Right,' said Steph. She scribbled a few last words on the paper, then folded it again. 'Superintendent, you take the lead on the Athenaeum, please. We'll work on the online records and the library. Nora, keep thinking and tell us if Mary turns up, either at the gardens or in your head.'

Nora saluted. 'Will do.' Then she looked puzzled. 'Can't you use your magic telephones to go online?'

Steph huffed. 'I'm not wrecking my eyes scrolling through a million records on my phone. That's a job for my laptop and a comfortable chair. If you do find out anything useful that can't wait, Nora, I order you to inform one of us at Erskine Street. Otherwise, we'll come here in the evenings or at the weekend.'

Nora pouted. 'I suppose that'll have to do. I mean, I know you're trying,' she said, possibly in response to my expression, 'but it's a long wait for us.'

'We're doing our best,' I said. 'But we've got real-life jobs as well.'

***

Steph and I were despondent when we walked into Erskine Street the next morning. Our activities after leaving the ghosts had been less than fruitful. I'd tried hunting for further information online, but every website seemed to require a subscription, and even if I did get a free trial, I wasn't great at searching at the best of times. Plus, to be honest, I was worried about what I might find. My easy ride as one of Sergeant Doughty's favourites hadn't prepared me for dealing with distressing facts.

In the end, I went to the library with Steph and secured a library card while she went to the archive section. However, all the Record Office appointments that day were taken and our stomachs were growling, so we took ourselves off for a late lunch, then decided to sleep on it.

'Maybe an idea will come to us today,' I said, as we signed in. 'Like when you're looking for something else and you find the thing you'd given up on.'

'Let's hope so,' said Steph, sounding unconvinced. But all hope was lost when we walked into the main office and saw Sergeant Doughty's face.

'Wondered when you two would roll in,' he said. 'Interview room three, *now*.'

Steph and I exchanged glances, then did as we were told.

Interview room three was a small, windowless room with strip lighting that made everyone look ghastly. Steph and I sat on the plastic chairs on one side of the small table. I thought about making small talk, then resolved to keep quiet in case the sergeant had bugged the room.

Five minutes later, by which time we were both as jittery as if we'd had a triple espresso each, Sergeant Doughty erupted into the room and shut the door smartly behind him. 'I suppose you two think you're clever, don't you?'

We said nothing. Any answer would have been wrong.

'Firstly, it was pretty sneaky of you to request leave

from two different superior officers. Not in the police spirit, given that we're shorthanded. As for the rest, you've been well and truly found out.'

'Sorry, sir?' said Steph.

'I imagine you'd like to know *how* I found out. Wouldn't you, Constable Saunders?'

I nodded. It seemed safest. If I spoke, I might let slip something he didn't already know.

'Had a call yesterday afternoon from my niece. Suzanna's a tour guide at St George's Hall, among other things. A hard worker, she is. She thought I'd be interested to hear that a Merseyside Police officer was disrupting her tour with silly, pointless questions. Naturally, I enquired the name of the officer, and when your name was mentioned, Constable Saunders, I wasn't remotely surprised. I assured Su that I would follow up on her complaint and asked her to check whether you were accompanied.' He looked at us both as if he'd found us on the bottom of his shoe. 'Did the pair of you really think you'd get away with such behaviour?'

'They were harmless questions, sir,' I said. 'For some reason, they're obsessed with ghost hunters at St George's Hall. They have a banned list and everything.'

'You do *not* bring the police force into disrepute by disrupting public services!' he shouted. 'You do *not* make a laughing stock of the force! Do I make myself clear?'

'Yes, sir,' we muttered.

'Count yourselves lucky that this stupid behaviour took place when you were off duty,' he said. 'As you have not contravened any written procedures, this reprimand will not go on your records.' Sergeant Doughty glared at us. 'However, as far as I am concerned, you are both on my watch list. I'd alternate the pair of you on every night and weekend shift for the whole of the next rota, but I don't trust you out of my sight. If either of you steps out of line so much as an *inch*… Be off with you!'

'Yes, sir,' we said, and got out of there as fast as we could.

'At least it wasn't official,' I said, as we hurried towards the main office.

'That doesn't matter, does it?' muttered Steph. Her words were light, but her tone certainly wasn't. And when I glanced her way, she was looking daggers at me.

CHAPTER 11

'It'll blow over,' said Mum, that evening.

'I hope so,' I said, as I stuck my fork into a large portion of macaroni cheese. 'It wasn't even my fault.'

'Really?'

'It wasn't! Those people were so suspicious. I was asking reasonable questions—'

'Which you knew would rattle their cage. If you didn't, you should have.'

'Aww, Muuum.' I ate a couple of forkfuls of pasta in moody silence. 'You're meant to be on my side.'

'I am,' she said, poking at her own plate with a fork. 'But I can see Steph's point. She's trying to keep her nose clean and you're dragging her into trouble by causing bother. If you'd kept quiet, that guide wouldn't have known your name and the sergeant wouldn't have kicked off at you, would he?'

I huffed. 'S'pose not. All right, I'll behave myself.'

'You will, Tash, if you know what's good for you.'

Mum gave me a severe look. 'Steph's keeping her career in mind and you should be, too.'

Obviously, I hadn't told Mum about Nora and the superintendent or any of the rest of it. She'd think I'd gone mad. Sometimes I wondered if Steph and I were victims of a joint hallucination, possibly brought on by the dodgy teabags at Erskine Street station.

So the next day, I got Steph alone in the kitchen at work and apologised. She heaved a weary sigh. 'Thanks,' she said. 'I'm pretty sure you won't stop getting me in trouble, but thanks for the thought.'

'Does that mean you're still on the case with us?' I asked, getting mugs from the cupboard.

'Do I have a choice?' I waited for a grin, or a nudge in the ribs to tell me that Steph didn't mind, but it didn't come.

I made tea, unsure how I felt about this. 'So you'll come to the Bridewell with me tonight?'

'Haven't decided.'

'Did you go last night?'

'No: I was still annoyed. With you, mostly. I didn't want to take it out on Nora or the superintendent.'

'Oh.' I put the milk in the fridge. 'I did say sorry.'

'Yes. But you didn't say you wouldn't do it again.'

I shut the fridge door a bit more firmly than I intended and faced her. 'Look, Steph, I'm new to all this. I'm not used to dealing with things I can't see or hear or even feel. I'm used to working on cases with facts and pieces of evidence. You can't expect me to adjust overnight, and I'm sorry if I'm not getting there as quickly as I should.' I gave my tea a stir and took it into the main office, then dropped into my chair and pulled the first of a large stack of folders from my in-tray.

When I finished work that night, I went straight to the Bridewell. Steph had dangled the keys in front of me before she left, which I took as confirmation that she wasn't ready to rejoin us yet. At least I managed to leave at a reasonable hour as I'd eaten at my desk, courtesy of a packed lunch from Mum.

I peeped through the gate and saw Nora and the superintendent in the yard. Both brightened when they saw me. 'Where have you been?' said Nora, then scowled, remembering that she was supposed to be cross with me.

'I stayed at my mum's last night,' I said. 'Steph and I had a – a small disagreement. The sergeant found out what we did on Monday and told us both off. So she's sulking.'

'That's not fair,' said Nora. 'Surely you can do what you want in your own time.'

'You'd think so, wouldn't you? Anyway, I'm here now.'

'You are,' said Superintendent Hicks. 'Although we won't be in half an hour or so.'

'*What?*'

'It's Athenaeum night,' said the superintendent, drawing himself up. 'If I remember rightly, Constable Sharpe tasked me with finding out as much as I could from the records of that fine institution.'

'She did.' I sighed and pushed my hair back. 'Sorry. I completely forgot it's Wednesday. I should have remembered.'

'It's because you're deep in the case,' said Nora, soothingly.

'I wish I was. At the moment, we've got so little information that I'm barely paddling.'

The superintendent chuckled. 'That's rather good.'

'Thank you. Unfortunately, it's also true. Have you two got any further with things?'

Both shook their heads.

'OK, well, we've got half an hour. Let's go to the file room and see what we can dig up.'

We went downstairs and looked at the mass of filing cabinets. 'Where do we start?' I murmured.

'That's the problem,' said Nora. 'We don't know.'

'There must be a way to narrow it down,' I said. 'The only things we know about Mary are her name and birth date. We don't even know if her baby was registered.'

'True,' said the superintendent. 'I'm not sure you had to, in those days. From what you've said, Mary was from a good family, so there would probably be a record of her somewhere. The baby…' He blew out his cheeks. 'It doesn't sound as if her parents would necessarily want the baby to be put on record.'

'Poor little thing.' I shuddered. 'I hope the baby didn't come to any harm.'

'Hopefully, it was adopted. Though that might not have been formal.'

'Yes, because that would help us. And we don't know why Mary's hanging out in the gardens. Yes, she's searching for her baby, but she said her parents sent her in a carriage and not to a hospital. So what else was there?'

'It wouldn't have been the courts or the concert hall,' said Superintendent Hicks. 'They weren't there.'

'That's so strange,' said Nora. 'I can't imagine a time when St George's Hall wasn't there.'

'Now you know how I feel when you talk about things like Lyons Corner Houses and random cemeteries,' I told her.

'And they wouldn't have sent her to the cemetery,' said the superintendent. He sat at the table and steepled his fingers. 'So what's left?'

'If I could get the internet working in here, maybe we'd get somewhere,' I said. Then I noticed Nora peering at the small collection of books stacked on the filing cabinets. 'What are you looking for?'

Nora turned. 'I wondered if there was a local history book here.'

'That would be convenient,' said the

superintendent, 'but very unlikely.' Nevertheless, we circled the room peering at book spines, just in case.

A horn bibbed outside and we all froze as if we were playing a party game. 'That's Inspector Farnsworth's car,' said Nora. 'What time is it?'

I checked the time on my phone: quarter to seven. 'He's early, but that isn't such a bad thing. Not when we want a local history reference.' I grinned. 'Keep him talking for a couple of minutes while I lock up.'

Nora saluted, but not in an unkind way, and they hurried off.

I made sure the building was secure, then ran round the corner to the inspector's bottle-green Volvo. He was in the driver's seat, naturally, with the superintendent next to him and the passenger-side window wound down. Nora was standing on the pavement, fiddling with her shoe.

'Inspector!' I called, and hurried over. 'Can I come too?'

He looked exasperated, which was unusual. 'I'm not a coach trip, Constable. I suppose this explains why Nora claims to have a ghost stone in her ghost shoe.' His eyes narrowed. 'Is this about that case? I'm aware that you and Constable Sharpe are not in Sergeant Doughty's good books.'

'We're not,' I said, opening the rear door and plonking myself down. 'The best way to fix that is to solve the case, so we can all move on. You're the perfect person to help. What was on the site of St George's Hall before it was built?'

Inspector Farnsworth started the car. 'Nora, are you getting in?' he called.

'Yup.' Nora walked round the car and slid through the door to sit next to me.

'I was in the process of explaining to these two that we can't stay at the Athenaeum for more than an hour tonight,' he said. 'Paperwork, and an early meeting tomorrow.'

'In that case, Inspector,' I said, 'I'll make the most of you while I've got you.'

He raised his eyebrows. 'Will you now.'

'Sir,' I added. 'If you wouldn't mind. As you love history and the past, I figured that this wouldn't feel like work.'

He laughed. 'If sheer cheek was a predictor of success in the police force, Tasha, you'd be an inspector already. To answer your question, before St George's Hall was built there was a church, a cemetery, a hospital, a seamen's hospital and a mill nearby. Oh, and a lunatic asylum.' We moved smoothly off.

Nora and I exchanged glances. 'Do you think…' I asked.

Nora gave a tiny shrug. 'It's possible.'

'You've given us a brilliant lead already, Inspector,' I said. 'I wonder if the Athenaeum has asylum records. And could you look someone up on one of your family tree websites for me?'

Inspector Farnsworth didn't speak as he navigated the maze of narrow roads behind the Bridewell. When we reached the junction with Prescot Street, he stopped the car and turned to me. 'Tasha, I've mentioned that I appreciate your tenacity.'

'Yes, sir.' I wasn't sure he had, but I wasn't about to contradict him. I had a feeling that I wouldn't like what came next.

'The only drawback is that if I give an inch, you'll take a yard. I'll agree to one thing, and before long you'll be popping your head round my office door with requests for just one more thing, or would I mind if…'

He sighed. 'You're perfectly correct – what you've outlined sounds exactly my sort of thing – but I absolutely, categorically, do not have time. Frankly, with things as they are politically, I would be a fool to get involved in this. So yes, I shall take you to the Athenaeum tonight and get you inside on a guest pass, and while you're there you are free to research what you like. But once I've dropped you at the Bridewell, I have to say, with regret, that you're on your own.'

The car turned left, and we moved into the traffic of the city evening.

CHAPTER 12

Inspector Farnsworth dropped us off outside the Bridewell just over an hour later. 'See you next week,' he said to the ghosts, who exited through the car doors. Then he turned to me. 'I expect I shall see you tomorrow, Constable Saunders.' I couldn't read his expression.

'Yes, sir,' I said, and got out.

'Wait a minute,' he said, as I was about to close the door. 'Isn't that Constable Sharpe?'

I followed his gaze. In the shadow of the doorway was Steph, looking uncomfortable.

I ran to her. 'You came!'

She smiled. 'I did, a few minutes ago. It was only when I knocked and no one answered that I realised tonight is Athenaeum night. I considered walking down, but then I wasn't sure if there'd be a pass for me, or whether you'd gone to St John's Gardens instead, or—'

'Can someone close the car door, please?' called Inspector Farnsworth.

I obliged, and the car moved off. Nora and the superintendent watched it go.

'Did he help you?' Steph asked.

'He answered a couple of questions. Apart from that, no: he wants to stay out of this. He said something about politics.' I decided not to mention his assessment of my character.

'So did you get any further?'

'We think Mary was possibly put in a lunatic asylum,' I said. 'That doesn't necessarily mean she had a mental health problem. From what I've read, families – or husbands – put women in asylums for all sorts of reasons. For Mary, being an unmarried mother could easily have been the reason.'

Steph looked stricken. 'Oh no. How awful.'

'It is. So now we need to track down the asylum records. I asked at the Athenaeum, but they didn't have any copies and never have done, so we don't even have ghost books to work from. We'll have to try the record office again.'

'If they do appointments outside office hours,' said Steph. 'I suppose I could email and ask if they have the records, as a starting point. But this doesn't get us anywhere with the other ghost.'

'It doesn't,' said Nora. 'Until we've sorted him out, the ghost hunters will keep bothering Mary.'

'If they still are,' I said. 'I think she's gone to ground. Who knows – maybe she's found her baby and gone to her rest.'

Nora shook her head. 'I meant to tell you earlier, but Inspector Farnsworth turned up before I got the chance. I had another vision and no, she hasn't. Mary's hiding, but I don't know where. And she still needs our help.'

'But what can we do?' asked Steph.

'We can go to St George's Hall,' said Nora. 'You can order me there.'

I looked at Steph, who shrugged. 'It's worth a go. We can't get much further without more information from Mary.'

'Then let's go,' said Superintendent Hicks.

'Umm...' Nora shifted from foot to foot as if she wanted to use the bathroom.

The superintendent eyed her. 'Is there a problem, Sergeant Norris?'

'Not a problem as such, but... In the vision I just had, Mary's hiding from a man, and—'

The superintendent stepped back. 'To be frank, I am far too senior to be out on the beat at this time of night. I was really offering in case you ladies required protection.'

I managed not to smile. 'We'll keep out of trouble, sir.'

'In that case, I shall maintain order at the

Bridewell.' He walked through the bars of the gate and pulled out his pipe.

***

The streets were still busy. People were spilling out of restaurants after taking advantage of early-bird menus, or heading into pubs for a drink.

'What could you see in your vision, Nora?' I asked.

'Well, Mary, obviously. She was surrounded by leaves and she was muttering to herself, saying things like "That nasty man must not find me. He says I won't find my little treasure, but I shall. Once *he* leaves me alone."'

'So she's probably still in the gardens,' I said. 'That's the only green space I can think of in the area.'

'Unless she's up a tree,' said Steph.

'She'd have to be able to climb it,' I said. 'Nora couldn't climb the scaffolding.'

'We'll see when we get there,' said Steph. 'Come on: it's too cold to be hanging about.'

At the entrance to the gardens, I stopped. 'I never thought – I'm in uniform. Mary doesn't like uniforms: they remind her of the attendants. That's why she won't talk to Nora.'

'Here.' Steph shrugged off her coat and gave it to me. 'Shall we split up and take opposite sides?'

'Good idea. She'll be wearing a plain brown dress

and no shoes.'

'I'll wait here,' said Nora, walking a little way into the gardens and sitting on a bench.

'Let's go,' said Steph, rubbing her arms.

I headed round the side of the gardens, peering into the vegetation and occasionally putting my hand into a bush. 'Mary,' I called softly. But I found nothing. *She isn't hiding from us too, is she? Who's this nasty man she's trying to avoid?* I had a sneaking feeling we'd have an interest in finding him, too.

Another bush investigated in vain, I turned to see where Steph had got to. She was a little further up her side than I was, bending to inspect another bush. I gazed around me at the trees. Could Mary be in one of those? It was possible, but—

A strange noise behind me made me jump. It sounded like a cross between a hiccup and a sob. I whipped round and Nora nearly ran into me. 'Tasha!' she wailed.

'Nora, what is it? What's wrong?' She was crying, but no tears were coming out. 'Is it Mary? Has something happened?'

'No, not Mary…'

I looked for Steph, but she was almost out of sight. 'I wish I could hug you, Nora, but it wouldn't work. Please tell me what's happened.'

'The other ghost…'

'You found him?' I frowned. 'He hasn't hurt you,

has he?'

Nora shook her head. 'I don't think that would be possible. But . . . yes. I didn't see him: I heard him. I felt a tickle, then he whispered, "Word in yer ear, miss." He told me he heard Superintendent Hicks plotting to get rid of me. "The old bloke in the posh suit," he said, but that must be the superintendent.'

'*What?*'

'Not now. When we were alive: when I was a matron and he was a detective. The man said he'd been in the Bridewell at the time, in one of the cells, and the superintendent joked about it with one of the sergeants.'

'He could be lying,' I said.

'I don't think so. He told me he recognised the superintendent when he was in the Great Hall with us the other day. He said he'd know that tone of voice anywhere, and he hadn't changed much. He said the superintendent used to have a long greatcoat. And he *did.*'

'Him and lots of other men, I expect.' I saw Steph coming back and waved at her to hurry. 'How could the superintendent get rid of you?'

'It's awful.' Nora covered her face with her hands. The ghost said that Detective Hicks – that's what he called him – he told the sergeant he'd have no peace while I was at the Bridewell and the sooner I was gone the better. The sergeant said something about women, then the superintendent said – he said I was the worst of the lot.' Her voice rose to a wail. 'I've never done a thing to him! I just wanted to do my duty and be a good policewoman!'

I sighed. 'We have to assume that the superintendent is innocent until proven guilty.' Nora looked extremely doubtful. 'However hard that is.'

Steph arrived, a little breathless. 'Have you found something?'

'Not in a good way.' I summarised what Nora had told me. 'But it does mean we know there's a ghost in the Great Hall, and he's mobile.'

'We'd better return to the Bridewell,' said Steph. 'I know where Nora's file is. Maybe that will give us some clues.'

Nora gasped. 'What if—'

'Don't worry,' I replied. 'If the superintendent bothers us, I'll bother *him.*'

It was a sombre walk back to the Bridewell. I hoped Superintendent Hicks was in his quarters. Whether we found evidence or not, any conversation with him was bound to be very difficult indeed.

'I don't understand,' Nora murmured, every so often.

'Try not to think about it, Nora,' said Steph. 'It's difficult, but dwelling on it won't help you. That ghost could just have been making mischief.'

'I know,' said Nora, 'but it still hurts.'

We reached the station, and Nora waited with us while Steph unlocked the door. 'Please don't leave me alone,' she said. 'I couldn't bear it.'

'We won't,' I told her. 'Are we going to the file room?'

'Yes,' said Steph.

'You will be quiet, won't you?' said Nora. 'The superintendent is probably in his quarters on the roof, but even so…'

We tiptoed into the station, and downstairs. It took Steph no more than a couple of minutes to find Nora's file. 'Here we are.' She set it on the table. 'Good thing we moved the personnel files from the locked cabinet when we cleared that paperwork last year.'

'He always scared me,' said Nora. 'It's only since Steph came to the station that he's begun to respect me. I kept out of his way. But I never thought…'

Steph turned the pages. 'Here we are,' she said. 'He complained that you were in the detective office on the third of March, 1917. Were you?'

Nora considered. 'I did sneak in sometimes, but I was always careful. He caught me once, or maybe twice.'

'There are several warnings here,' said Steph. 'You got a final written warning for going missing while on duty, just before you went off sick with the flu.'

'I probably did,' said Nora. 'I tried so hard. I wanted to help. Somehow, whatever I did wasn't right.

When was that?'

'Late June: the twenty-sixth.'

'June...' Nora paced, frowning. 'Oh my word!' She stopped dead. 'I remember! I was taking tea to the detective offices when I heard someone say that they needed someone to keep watch on a local jeweller's shop, as there'd been a report of a possible robbery at lunchtime, but all the men were out. I wasn't eavesdropping: the door was open. I knew that if I offered they'd never let me go, so I delivered the tea and headed out. I kept that shop under close observation for three hours and nothing happened – and when I came back I was for it. And when I told the superintendent why I'd done it, both the detectives in that office – one was Detective Hicks, of course – denied ever saying a thing like it.' Her fists clenched. 'Oh, I could—'

I held up a hand. 'Did you hear that tapping?'

Nora froze. 'It isn't *him*, is it?'

'No. Someone's knocking on the front door.'

We listened. There it was again, and a voice calling 'Hello?'

'That's the inspector,' said Steph. She looked at me. 'I'd better let him in.'

'Well yeah, we can't leave him outside,' I said. 'I'm pretty sure that would be a disciplinary matter. He doesn't sound cross, anyway.'

Steph went upstairs. Soon, we heard the release of

the door catch and the inspector's voice. 'I imagine Tasha has filled you in on what I said earlier. I meant it at the time, but I was thinking of it all the way home.' Their steps grew closer.

'We've got a bit of a problem, Inspector,' said Steph.

'Well, hopefully, with my local history knowledge and help from online records, we can get somewhere.' The door to the file room opened and Inspector Farnsworth stepped in. 'Hello, everyone,' he said, smiling. 'Is the superintendent having an early night?'

'He's not invited,' I said. 'Nora's been tipped off about something he did when they were both alive, and we're in the process of investigating.'

'Oh.' The inspector's eyebrows drew together. 'Oh dear. Perhaps one of you can fill me in, if you wouldn't—'

Click.

We all heard it: the click of a lock, followed by the creak of the front door swinging open.

'What's going on?' I said.

'Someone's come in,' said Steph. 'Someone with a key.'

'But—'

'Shhh.'

We waited. Measured footsteps paced from room to room. *If they go up to the detective office, maybe we could make a run for it.*

They didn't. We heard squeaks and creaks as whoever it was came downstairs. I glanced at Inspector Farnsworth, whose mouth was set in a firm line.

Steph's hand found mine.

The footsteps advanced, then stopped.

Nora scrambled under the table.

The file-room door opened, but whoever was behind it didn't peep round. After what seemed an eternity, Sergeant Doughty strolled into the room. 'Well, well, well,' he said, surveying us with a gleam in his eye. 'What a surprise.'

CHAPTER 13

Sergeant Doughty pulled out a chair and sat down at the file-room table. 'So,' he said, 'what do you two have to say for yourselves?'

Steph seemed to have turned to stone. 'I – I—'

'They're here under my orders,' said Inspector Farnsworth, and I shot him a grateful look. 'Therefore, Sergeant, you should be speaking to me. I'd be interested to know what brings you here at this time of night.'

Sergeant Doughty smiled the smile of someone who had their story all worked out. 'A concerned resident rang the station saying that they'd seen lights on at the Bridewell and they were worried. I happened to be working late and took the call. Naturally I came over straight away, since any threat to police property is very serious. Even when it's a knackered old dump like this. But when I saw your car outside, Inspector, I realised that far from needing to worry about burglars, vandals or arsonists, I should expect an after-hours get-together.'

'May I remind you, Sergeant, that you take your orders from me?' Inspector Farnsworth's tone was mild, but I could detect a steely core.

'Oh, I do, Inspector,' cooed the sergeant. 'But I imagine the chief inspector would be interested to know what's been going on here. Is this a regular thing, by any chance? A little Wednesday rendezvous, invitees only? What do you get up to, I wonder?'

'Is it any of your business?' countered Inspector Farnsworth. But though he was unquestionably the senior officer in the room, somehow the balance of power had shifted. He was doing his best, but he was on the back foot.

'Let me see…' Sergeant Doughty peered at Nora's file, still open on the table. 'An old personnel file: what on earth could you want with that? Should it even be here? I'd have to check the schedule, of course, but I'm pretty sure this should have been chucked out, given how ancient it looks. And an open filing cabinet. Oh dear, not very good data protection, is it? And the fact that I could just walk into the file room…' He tutted. 'I wonder what the Chief will think?'

'Go ahead,' said Inspector Farnsworth. 'Phone him now, if you like. I'm sure he won't mind being disturbed at home.'

Sergeant Doughty's eyes glittered. 'Oh, this can wait until office hours.' He took a notebook from his pocket and scribbled in it with a silver pencil. 'I'll give you a minute or two to clear up, then I shall see you off the premises. Don't even think about taking anything with you.' He got up and strolled out.

'Thank you, Inspector,' I said.

'Don't mention it,' said Inspector Farnsworth.

I nudged Steph, but she seemed in a daze. 'That's it,' she said. 'He'll send me back to Cheshire for sure. That's if they'll take me, after what he'll tell them. I only ever wanted to be a police officer…'

Nora crawled out from under the table. A cobweb had attached itself to her hat and bobbed behind her. 'What am I going to do?' she said, as she got to her feet. 'You can't leave me on my own with him. Not knowing what I do. Maybe you think it isn't true, but I *know*.'

'Don't worry,' I said, wishing more than ever that I could give her a hug. 'We'll sort things out somehow.' I wanted to be specific, but I didn't know how much Sergeant Doughty could hear. Knowing him, he probably had his ear to the door.

'Come on,' said Inspector Farnsworth, 'let's get this file put away. We can't do any more here.' But as he said it, he was taking pictures of the open pages with his phone.

'The inspector's right,' I said.

'It doesn't make it any easier, though,' said Steph. She studied Nora thoughtfully, then leaned forward and cupped her hand to Nora's ear. 'I order you to accompany me to my flat,' she whispered.

Nora's eyes widened and she turned to Steph. 'Really?'

Steph nodded, then closed the file and put it in the cabinet. 'Let's go.'

Sergeant Doughty appeared in the doorway and Nora dived behind me. 'Before you do, one of you must have a key. Given the amount of time you've spent idling here, Constable Sharpe, I assume it's you.'

'Sorry, Sergeant,' said Steph, pulling out the pockets of her jeans. 'Not this time.' She sounded like someone who's run out of lives, making a last stand.

The sergeant took a step towards her. 'You'd better not be lying—'

'I've got them, Sergeant,' I said, taking the keys from my pocket. 'I suppose you want me to hand them over.'

'Given that you should never have had them in the first place, yes I do.' He held out his palm and I dropped the key ring into it. I couldn't bear the thought of touching him. 'Any other illicit keys or belongings? If I discover them later, it will be much worse for you.' He spoke with the confidence of someone who knows they will not be challenged.

'No keys, sir,' I said.

'Me neither,' said Steph.

'I don't have a key either,' said Inspector Farnsworth. 'And strangely, when I headed to Erskine Street station a few minutes ago to fetch the keys, they weren't there. Neither were you, Sergeant.'

'We must have missed each other,' said Sergeant Doughty. 'Now, if you don't mind, some of us have work to do. Reports to write, recommendations to make. That sort of thing.' He couldn't keep the grin off his face. 'I'm sure getting this place off our hands would make a few cost savings.'

I did my best to maintain a poker face, as did Steph. Nora looked as if she was bursting to say something, but settled for shaking her fist at the sergeant. I suspect she was worried about swearing in front of Inspector Farnsworth.

We trooped out under the sergeant's eye and he followed us up the stairs. As far as possible, Nora kept out of the sergeant's line of sight, though I'm not sure why she bothered. It wasn't as if the sergeant could see her.

'I'll leave you to lock up, Sergeant Doughty,' said Inspector Farnsworth. 'I daresay you'll enjoy that.' He turned to us. 'I'll give you a lift home. It's the least I can do in the circumstances.'

'Thank you, sir,' Steph and I chorused, and Nora nodded vigorously.

Once we were in the car, with Nora sitting between Steph and me, Steph gave the inspector her address. I had what felt like a million questions, but working out where to start – and what to say without being rude – was the problem. Steph seemed to be lost in gloom, and Nora was gazing out of the window. So we were some way clear of the Bridewell when I finally found my voice. 'What's going on exactly, sir?' I asked. 'I mean, obviously it's up to you and I'm not questioning your actions in any way, but why the heck did you let the sergeant throw his weight around like that?'

'I feel like a taxi driver or a chauffeur,' said Inspector Farnsworth. 'What with you three squashed together in the back.'

'We were going to let Nora sit in front, but she kind of dived in,' I replied.

Nora's lip wobbled dangerously.

'I'm only joking, Nora,' I assured her. 'But seriously, *why*, sir?'

'You'll remember I mentioned politics earlier, Tasha, when I was excusing myself from helping you.'

I nodded, then realised he couldn't see me. Or hopefully not, since he was driving. 'Yes, sir.'

'That's part of it. Sergeant Doughty, whom I inherited when I moved to Erskine Street, has never forgiven me for taking what he sees as his job. He's served his time – more than his time, indeed – he's passed the exam, but he has never secured an inspector's position.' He paused. 'Probably because he's a complete weasel, and everybody knows it. That's confidential, by the way,' he added, as Steph and I burst out laughing.

'I appreciate your honesty, sir,' I said, once I'd calmed myself down, 'but that still doesn't explain it.'

'Ah, the famous Saunders tenacity.' He sighed. 'I'm coming to it. The sergeant has been trying a new tactic. Namely, cosying up to the Chief and making himself useful. Recommendations for budget savings, corners we could cut, that sort of thing. One of the things that hasn't escaped Sergeant Doughty's sharp eye is that I have reached an age when I could, potentially, retire.'

'Oh,' said Steph and I, together.

'You can't be that old, Inspector,' said Nora.

'Thank you for the compliment, Nora.' I could hear the smile in his voice. 'But it's true. I could, of course, carry on for a good few years yet. However, for Sergeant Doughty's purposes, he would much rather I went as soon as possible. It appears that his plan is to whisper in the Chief's ear that my mind is clearly not on my job and that he should have a word with me about making a graceful exit, leaving the field clear for the sergeant to step up. Since he's made himself so useful, it's possible that the Chief will listen to him. I mean, think of the cost savings.' The last sentence could have soured a pint of milk.

'You *can't* go, sir,' I said. 'You can't leave us with Sergeant Doughty in charge. He's bad enough as it is. Imagine what he'd be like as an inspector.'

'I'm aware of that,' said Inspector Farnsworth. 'And I dislike the idea almost as much as you do. Unfortunately, catching us at the Bridewell tonight might be just what he needs to seal the deal.'

'What a mess,' said Steph. 'What a horrible, horrible mess. And all we were trying to do was help.' She rubbed her cheek and turned to the window, and we drove through the streets in silence.

CHAPTER 14

'Is this right?' asked Inspector Farnsworth, as he pulled up outside Steph's apartment block.

'Yes. Thank you.' Steph's hand moved towards the seatbelt release button. 'Unless... Unless you'd like to come in?'

'Well, I could...' he mused. 'Is there somewhere to leave the car?'

'Yes, there are parking spaces round the back.' She paused. 'I'm really sorry about earlier, Inspector. We never meant for you to get in trouble.'

Inspector Farnsworth laughed softly. 'I'm not in trouble, Steph. Not yet, anyway.' He drove round the corner and into the car park, looking this way and that for a space. 'Aha, here we are.' He swung the car round and reversed in. 'Right. Lead the way, Steph.'

'So you have a flat, Steph,' said Nora. 'Which floor is it on?'

'The second,' Steph replied.

'Can we take the lift? I haven't ridden in a lift for ages.'

'I don't see why not,' said Steph. I was just relieved that Nora was more like her usual cheerful self.

Steph let us into the lobby. For once, the lift was working. 'I wish I could push the button,' said Nora. 'When I was a girl, if ever we went to a department store, Ma used to lift me up so I could do it.'

The lift pinged. 'Was that it? That didn't take long.' She looked disappointed.

'I'm afraid the flat isn't tidy,' said Steph. 'I wasn't expecting visitors.' However, when she opened the door, the flat was its usual bare self, apart from a used plate, a fork and a glass by the sink in the kitchenette.

'Wow,' said Nora, turning slowly. 'Is this all yours?'

Steph gazed around the small flat with a smile. 'I rent it. But yes. Unless Tasha's here, of course.'

'Oh yes,' said Nora. 'So will you move in, Tasha?'

'Um, that's up to Steph,' I said. 'I just stay over sometimes.' Trust Nora to drop a bombshell without warning.

Nora wandered round the flat. 'What's that?' she asked, pointing to the television. 'Is it a screen, like on your magic telephone?'

'That's a TV, for watching programmes and films and things,' said Steph. 'I suppose it is a bit like a big phone.'

'Thought so.' Nora stood for a while, then moved on, inspecting the sofa, the rug, the blinds. 'It's very you,' she said.

'I'll take that as a compliment,' Steph replied. 'Tea, coffee? The coffee will be instant.'

'Tea, please,' said Inspector Farnsworth. 'I'd love a coffee, but so would my insomnia.'

'Tea for me, too,' I said, to show solidarity, even though I slept like a log.

Steph went to the kitchenette and filled the kettle.

'So what happens now?' said Nora. 'What do we do?'

'The sergeant won't do anything tonight,' said the inspector. 'Well, he'll probably gloat and possibly rehearse his speech for tomorrow. However, I happen to know that the Chief's at a conference all day, so the sergeant will have to wait.'

'Good,' I replied, and the viciousness of my tone startled me.

Inspector Farnsworth raised his eyebrows. 'I'll make sure I stay on the right side of you, Tasha.'

'Sorry. It's so annoying, though. It's not even as if we're doing this in work hours. It's none of Sergeant Doughty's business.'

'He's choosing to make it his business,' said the inspector. 'I imagine he'll say we were misusing police resources for private purposes. Dereliction of duty, or similar. Maybe I'm sentimental, but don't we have a duty to the dead, as well as the living? No one else can do what we do.'

'While we're speaking of that, sir,' said Nora, 'will you – would you mind talking to Superintendent Hicks?' She looked more uncomfortable than I had ever seen her. 'I don't want to go back to the Bridewell, but I can't stay here for ever. Although it is very nice,' she said, in Steph's direction.

'Yes, what is all this about the superintendent?'

'Tasha, will you tell the inspector?' said Nora. She went to the sofa and wedged herself into the corner.

It wasn't as if I had an option, so I summarised the problem as briefly as possible.

'I see,' said Inspector Farnsworth, gravely. 'Yes, Nora, I shall visit the Bridewell and see what Superintendent Hicks has to say on the matter. And I shall also check the files.' He crossed the room and sat in the armchair. 'While I shall not take sides on this until I have more evidence, I have a couple of observations.'

Steph brought through a tray. 'Here we go,' she said. 'Nora, I know you can't drink it, but I made you a brew anyway.' She put one mug on the side table beside Nora.

'For me?' Nora leaned over as if she was inhaling the steam. 'Ooh, it's lovely and hot!' She beamed at us.

I took my own mug and sat next to Nora. 'So, what

are your observations, sir?'

'Firstly, we don't know whether this ghost is telling the truth or twisting things for his own reasons.' Nora, looking indignant, opened her mouth to speak, but he held up a finger. 'I'm still not taking sides. Secondly, according to the scenario this ghost describes, he was alive when you and the superintendent were both working at the Bridewell.'

My mouth dropped open. 'You're right. We've been so busy trying to get at the truth of what happened that we completely missed it.'

'So what you're saying,' said Steph, 'is that there might be a record of this man at the Bridewell.'

'Unless we got rid of it when we did that big purge of records at the end of last year,' I said. 'Oh heck.'

'No, but I set up that spreadsheet, remember? How long were you at the Bridewell, Nora?'

'September 1917 to June 1919,' said Nora, immediately.

'That's nowhere near as long as I thought,' I commented.

'That's Spanish flu for you,' said Nora. 'Flaming pandemic.'

Steph began to get up, then paused. 'My laptop's at work.'

'Mine isn't,' said Inspector Farnsworth, with a grin. He pulled a slim laptop from his work bag. 'Let's see what we can find.' He huddled over the laptop, his long fingers stroking the trackpad. 'Here we go: Bridewell records, and the fields are file date, offender's surname and first name, nature of crime, date of crime, officer in charge, case resolved or not. Lovely.'

We got up and stood behind the inspector, peering over his shoulder. 'This is what we have between those dates.' He highlighted a large chunk of rows, then created a new sheet and pasted them in. 'We can take out the women – not that there are many…' He deleted a few rows. 'Which leaves us with this.'

'That's still a lot of people,' said Steph.

'Agreed. But before this, we had no guidance and a huge pool of possibles, if you consider the cemetery alone.' He scrolled through the list. 'As the superintendent was a detective, it's likely that he had the conversation which our ghost overheard during the day. That suggests the ghost wasn't just kept overnight. Therefore, he was in for something more serious than drunkenness or begging.'

'Yes,' said Nora. 'When I was at the station, beggars only got arrested late in the evening, either to fill up the cells or to make sure they had a roof over their heads for the night.'

'Exactly,' said Inspector Farnsworth. 'If this person was picked up for a serious offence, he would have stood trial at Liverpool assizes, which leads us back to—'

'St George's Hall!' I exclaimed.

'Yes. So our next job is to take out the names of anyone who was kept in for what was considered a minor offence.' The inspector started to delete rows. 'This looks more promising,' he murmured.

'How does that relate to the ceiling of the Great Hall?' I asked.

'Good question, Tasha,' said the inspector.

'If the ceiling repairs have been stopped,' said Steph, 'that's presumably what the ghost wants. Why?'

'I shall hazard a guess,' said Inspector Farnsworth. 'Something's up there that they don't want found. Presumably, they put it there. So our next question is, when did anyone last do anything to the plasterwork of the Great Hall?'

'I'll do a search,' I said, pulling out my phone.

'Me too,' said Steph.

Our thumbs flew over our phones. 'It's not a race, you two,' said Nora. But in our minds, it was.

'Got it!' said Steph. 'Plasterwork repairs were done in 1896, ready for Queen Victoria's Diamond Jubilee celebrations. And minor repairs were undertaken in the late 1940s.'

Something clicked in my brain. 'I wonder… When I saw her first, Mary mentioned a woman with servants looking for a necklace. Apparently she said the thief might have dropped it. She was wearing a frilly dress and a big hat with a real bird on it.'

The inspector groaned.

'What?' I asked. 'That's a good lead.'

'It is, but it means I'll have to research ladies' fashions. Thanks for nothing, Tasha.'

'My pleasure,' I replied, with a grin.

'For now, back to our spreadsheet. Assuming that our ghost did hide an item in the ceiling, we need a list of the people who worked on it.' He pondered for a moment. 'I'll try the British Newspaper Archive.' He clicked a tab at the bottom of the screen, logged in, and typed *St George's Hall Liverpool Great Hall roof* in the search box. 'Several results, a couple from 1896, and one has a photo.' He clicked to reach the article, then on the photo, which enlarged to show two rows of men in working clothes, standing stiffly. A few were beaming, some stared straight ahead with expressionless faces, a handful looked embarrassed. Underneath was a caption: *The team repairing the plasterwork at St George's Hall.* 'Behold, a list of names! So now we search our spreadsheet.' He brought the spreadsheet up and opened the search box. 'Williams, yes, but not Joseph... Keating, but not John... Arbuthnot . . . no. Wales . . . no. Ainscough . . . Ronald . . . yes! The spreadsheet says that he was arrested for mugging an old lady and sent on to Walton Jail two days later.'

'I remember that,' said Nora. 'I overheard Sergeant

Thomas talking about it in the break room. He said he was a proper villain: an old gang man. We kept him longer because Walton were waiting for a cell to come free. They were worried he'd corrupt anyone he shared a cell with.'

'Well,' said Inspector Farnsworth, 'that is interesting.' He returned to the newspaper archive window and typed *Ronald Ainscough High Rip Gang* in the search box. '*High Rip caught in the act*,' he read. '*Tuesday 28th July, 1885. Three members of the notorious High Rip Gang were convicted of assault and robbery at Liverpool Assizes. Christopher Lamb, 24, Robert Payne, 23, and Ronald Ainscough, 17, received seven, five and two years respectively, all with hard labour.*'

'Wow,' I said. 'Well done, Inspector. That was pretty smooth.'

'One tries.' He looked round at us. 'Of course, I shall do my due diligence and double check the names left in this spreadsheet, in case anyone else fits the bill, but I'm pretty sure that we have our man, if the ghost was telling the truth. I'll also follow up your lead on the necklace and the frilly woman, Tasha. Then, like the good sergeant, I shall also seek a meeting.'

Steph and I exchanged glances. 'With Adam?' I said.

The inspector nodded. 'Oh yes.'

CHAPTER 15

'Should I get changed?'

Steph laughed. 'Tasha, I don't think I've ever seen you so nervous. You weren't this bothered last time.'

'No. I didn't know what I was getting into then, and I do now. More or less.'

'To be honest, I wasn't sure, since this is out of hours,' said Steph, 'but I figure that we're there with Inspector Farnsworth on police business. Plus, we'll look more official and less like ghost hunters.'

'And I'm in uniform,' said Nora, 'so you can keep me company.'

'True.' I inspected myself in the mirror and put my hat on. 'OK, I guess I'm ready.'

'Good,' said Steph. 'Because we'll need to crack on to get to St George's Hall in time.'

Thursday had been tense, to say the least. Sergeant Doughty had done his best impression of a thundercloud in uniform that morning, possibly having discovered that the Chief wasn't available. Both Steph and I had found our in-trays groaning with paper when we came in. However, Inspector Farnsworth had made a point of leaving his door open and coming into the main office every so often to chat to people. Maybe he was looking for support, but I suspected he wanted to take his mind off things.

My phone buzzed at a quarter past eleven. Steph's did too. Normally, one of us would have been out on the beat at this time, but today we were in too much disgrace to be let out of the office. Not that our fellow officers noticed: they were too glad to escape the eagle eye of the sergeant.

I waited a few minutes, then slipped the phone in my pocket. 'Anyone for a drink?'

Several hands went up, and I went to the kitchen to read my message in peace.

St GH steps tonight 7.45. AF on board. I didn't recognise the number: probably the inspector's personal mobile. *I've got the inspector's private number*, I thought, and I couldn't help smiling. *Take that, Sergeant Doughty.* I put the phone away and filled the kettle.

The day dragged, filled as it was with tasks so mind-numbingly dull that I suspected Sergeant Doughty saved them for special occasions. Maybe he was hoping we'd both resign from frustration. But I got on with them, and so did Steph.

As the afternoon wore on, I found myself getting twitchy. *AF on board* meant Adam Fagan would be there. Prison warder/historian at HMP Liverpool by day, and also a summoner of spirits. I wondered what else he could do, and shivered. *I'd rather not know.*

'Are you all right?' Steph whispered, when the sergeant was out of the room.

'Yeah, fine.'

'You're not. You look as if you'd hit the ceiling if someone so much as dropped a pen.'

Trust Steph to pick up on it. 'OK,' I said, 'I'm a bit nervous about later. About Adam. I didn't know last time that he's…'

'Sort of immortal?'

'Yes.'

'You managed fine with Nora. It's not that different.'

'I suppose.' But I resolved to keep my distance. I hoped Adam's sort of immortality wasn't catching.

And here we were, walking to meet him. Town was busy, but the area around the hall was quiet now that everything was closed.

'Look, there they are,' Nora said, pointing. Inspector Farnsworth was standing at the top of the steps, between two pillars. Beside him was a tall, slightly stooped figure, his white hair in a ponytail and dressed in dark clothes. The shadows cast by the old-fashioned street lamps didn't help. I did my best not to shudder.

'Come on,' said Steph. 'They aren't the people you should worry about.'

'I know.' I was still the last to reach them.

'Good evening,' said Adam, with a sort of half bow which I imagined he had learnt many, many years ago. 'Are we ready?' He turned to Inspector Farnsworth. 'I believe you said our appointment was for eight o'clock.'

'That's right,' said the inspector. 'The cleaners will be finished and all the staff gone. Except for the person who's letting us in, of course. Do you have the details?'

'I do.' Adam patted his pocket. 'I must admit that I'm intrigued. For such an interesting site, stories of ghosts here are remarkably few.'

'Probably because of the management,' I muttered.

Inspector Farnsworth checked his watch. 'I make it five to. Shall we head round?'

We trooped to the side entrance. I expected the inspector to knock, but instead, he took out his phone and texted. 'She shouldn't be long,' he said.

As we waited, I looked for CCTV cameras. What if we were caught? This was very cloak and dagger, not the official welcome I had expected. But where St George's Hall was concerned, I was learning to expect the unexpected.

After what seemed like an hour, but could only

have been a couple of minutes, we heard muffled noises followed by a click. One of the doors opened to reveal a small, plumpish woman with fluffy brown hair, wearing the regulation white blouse and dark skirt. Her name tag said *Sue Marsden*. 'Hello,' she said. 'You'd better come in.'

As we filed in, I realised. 'You're her,' I said. 'The woman who led the tour when people heard the noises.'

'Yes, that's right,' she said, sounding harried. 'I'd rather not talk about it, if you don't mind.'

I frowned. 'I thought you said it was just the building.'

She actually shuddered. 'I didn't say that. That was the comms team. I was absolutely bricking myself. Haven't done a tour since. It's a relief, to be honest. I usually felt a bit funny in the Great Hall, even if nothing strange was going on.'

'Oh no, I'm so sorry,' I said. 'Goes to show you shouldn't believe everything you read.'

Inspector Farnsworth stepped forward. 'Hopefully, Ms Marsden—'

'Oh, do call me Sue. Everyone does.'

'Thank you, Sue. Hopefully, we shall put to rest whatever is making the strange noises and you won't be troubled again.'

'That would be wonderful.' She gazed doubtfully at the inspector. 'I'm assuming you're Inspector

Farnsworth, but who are all these other people?'

'I do apologise, I should have introduced everyone. In no particular order, these are Constable Steph Sharpe, Constable Tasha Saunders, and Mr Adam Fagan, who is an expert in these matters.'

The faint line between Sue Marsden's eyebrows deepened. 'Who is the other lady?'

Nora looked ready to burst with happiness. 'I'm Sergeant Nora Norris. Pleased to meet you!' And she saluted.

Sue seemed rather taken aback. 'Er, would you like some tea before you start? Will this take long?'

'It's hard to say,' said Inspector Farnsworth. 'There is a distinct possibility that we may not be successful at our first attempt, but I promise we'll do our best. And no, we won't need tea. So if you don't mind leading the way to the Great Hall...'

'You don't expect me to stay and watch, do you?' Sue's eyes were round as blue marbles.

'You may, if you wish to.'

'I'll wait outside,' she said firmly. 'This way.'

The walk to the Great Hall was surprisingly short. In my mind, I'd imagined the full circuit of the tour. 'Here we are,' said Sue. 'I'll put the lights on and get out of your way.' She darted in, flipped various switches and dashed out. 'I'll be in the corridor.' I suspected she'd be some way down it.

'Well, here we are,' said the inspector, gazing

around him.

'Yes,' said Adam. Now that we were in full light, I saw he was wearing an old-fashioned dark suit with a knitted tie. It would probably have fetched a fortune in a vintage shop. He took a piece of paper from his jacket pocket and unfolded it. 'Are we ready?'

As if on cue, a scratching noise came from somewhere in the roof, behind the scaffolding.

'It's as well Sue isn't here,' said the inspector, 'but something is.'

'Indeed,' said Adam. 'If you wouldn't mind standing back.' We all took a few steps away from him.

Adam held up his hand. 'Ronald Ainscough, you are wanted for questioning regarding various crimes of robbery and violence undertaken with the High Rip Gang. Show yourself!'

Silence for a few seconds, then a low, dirty laugh. It echoed around the hall until it felt as if every member of that long-dead gang was laughing at us. My fists clenched.

'I don't think that's specific enough,' said Inspector Farnsworth.

'Very well.' Adam consulted his sheet, then raised his hand again. 'Ronald Ainscough, I summon you to my presence concerning what is hidden in the ceiling of this building. Show yourself!'

This time, the horrible, raucous laughter followed

immediately. I grabbed Steph's hand. Poor Nora, unable to do the same, hugged herself.

'Oh dear,' said Adam. 'We've drawn a blank.'

'Unless…' Inspector Farnsworth was frowning slightly, and there was an odd set to his mouth. 'I searched the newspaper archives for anything stolen on the premises close to the time when Ronald Ainscough worked here. It seemed a distant possibility – too much of a coincidence, if anything – but perhaps… Would you mind if I tried?'

Adam's eyebrows shot up. 'Of course not, Inspector. You've seen me do this a few times, so you know the form of words. If it doesn't work, I can always—'

Inspector Farnsworth raised his hand and marched forward until he was at the foot of the scaffolding. 'Ronald Ainscough, I command you to appear regarding the theft of Lady Huyton's emerald necklace on Saturday the twenty-fifth of July, 1896. Show yourself!'

This time, there was no laughter. But none of us thought the strange presence had left. Something hung in the air: a damp, close sensation. The air smelt musty, with a faint whiff of metal and polish, like the smell of a knife which was well cared for and kept sharp.

'He's coming,' said Nora. 'Look.'

I followed her pointing finger. At the foot of the

scaffolding, a blur was sharpening into a small, bent man. Strands of thin greyish-white hair straggled down to his collar, and his weatherbeaten face was as wrinkled as a rotting apple. 'What you want?'

'You know what I want,' said Inspector Farnsworth. 'Where did you put that necklace?'

'I've kept it safe for years and years,' said Ronald Ainscough. 'What makes you think I'll tell you?'

'Because you're stuck here until you do,' said the inspector. 'From what I've read about you, you spent over half your life in prison. This is grander than any prison I've ever seen, but you still can't leave, can you?'

'Plenty worse places,' the ghost replied. 'What's in it for me if I tell you?'

'Peace,' said the inspector. 'Rest, eventually. Freedom, perhaps.'

'Overrated, freedom is,' the ghost observed. 'I've minded that jewel all these years. Why should anyone else have it? What have they done to deserve it?'

'But *you* don't have it,' I said. 'You can't get at it and you can't do anything with it. So it's no one's. You might as well have thrown it away.'

'Throw it away, a fine piece like that?' He looked horrified, then leered at me. 'You're a fine piece too, missy.'

'Don't you dare speak to her like that!' Steph shouted.

'All right, keep your hair on. I was paying 'er a compliment. Anyway, far as I was concerned, it was only gonna be here tempory, till the dust settled.' He chortled. 'Had it off the silly woman's neck before she knew what'd hit 'er. The next day I wrapped it in a rag, put it in the plaster and slapped on a couple more layers, ready for the master moulder to put his frills and furbelows on top. Did a lovely job, he did. Shame to mess it up, though I would have done. Got thrown off the job first. Foreman caught me nicking his lunch a few days later and gave me my marching orders. Stupid, really: that necklace would've paid for all my meals for the rest of my life, probably. Still, we live and learn.'

'Were you still with the High Rip Gang when you stole it?' I asked.

'Like hell I was. That first prison sentence knocked the gang stuff right out of me. If that great lunk Chris Lamb hadn't fallen over when we was running off, we wouldn't have been taken up. Couple of passers-by grabbed him, then he turned us in to get time off his sentence, the sneak. Bob and I made sure he got sorted out in prison, though.' He gave an evil chuckle. 'From that day on, I decided I'd be my own master. Didn't always work out, but at least it was on my own terms.'

'Now you've got a chance to make amends on your own terms,' said the inspector. 'You've already admitted you stole the necklace, so you may as well tell us where it is.'

YES, boomed a voice which came from everywhere at once.

'Flipping 'eck!' Ronald Ainscough stared all around him.

INDEED, RONALD AINSCOUGH. FLIPPING HECK, AS YOU SAY.

The ghost looked as if his eyes would pop out of his head. 'I've seen and heard things in my time, but that's a new one.'

YOU HAVE COME TO YOUR RECKONING, MR AINSCOUGH. YOU SEEM LIKE A MAN WITH A GREAT DEAL TO SAY.

'Oh, I could tell you some stories. Is this like the bit in court where you ask for other offences to be taken into consideration?'

There was silence for a moment. *IN A MANNER OF SPEAKING, YES.*

'First of all, the necklace is behind the panel with the royal coat of arms on it. Right in the middle. Now, the pigs caught me ten times, but I reckon there's another thirty times they didn't. So three quarters of the time I got off scot-free, which is a pretty good record if you ask me…' His voice was starting to fade, and his clothing had already blurred. 'So when I left prison that first time, I fell in with this woman. She was a one, and no mistake…'

And then he was gone.

'I actually feel sorry for Justice, or Judgement, or whatever that voice is,' said Steph. 'I reckon that guy will keep them busy for some time.'

'Yes,' said Inspector Farnsworth. 'Think of the crimes that will be cleared up.' He studied his right hand. 'I almost wish I could hear it all, and amend the files—'

'Wait!' cried Nora. 'Justice! Bring him back!'

Ronald Ainscough popped into view, looking irritated. 'What? I was just getting into my stride.'

'Why did you tell me what the superintendent said?' Nora asked. 'I know it was you. I recognise your voice.'

'Yeah, I'll admit to that.' Ronald Ainscough considered. 'To be perfickly honest with you, I'm not sure. Probably because I saw you trying to help that young woman who's always wandering. She won't find that kid of hers and I've told her as much, but it's kind of you. You seem a good sort, and I knew that superintendent you're friendly with was a right so-and-so behind your back. So I thought, well, it don't hurt me and fair dos. Maybe it'll give me extra credit with him upstairs.' He winked.

'Thank you,' said Nora. 'I think. You may go now.'

'Always happy to help a lady,' said Ronald Ainscough, with an unspeakable leer, and vanished.

'Well,' said Adam, 'I suppose that concludes our

business for tonight.'

'Not quite,' said Inspector Farnsworth. 'We need to tell Sue what we discovered, and that she doesn't have to worry about the noises any more.' He crossed the room and opened the door. 'Sue!' he called. 'We're finished.'

A minute later, Sue's head appeared. 'Did you—Oh!' She walked into the room, taking it in as if she'd never seen it before. 'It smells so fresh and clean!' She beamed at Inspector Farnsworth. 'Thank you so much!'

Inspector Farnsworth smiled back at her. 'Would you like to hear about the discovery we've made?'

Sue tore herself away from her surroundings. 'Oh, yes, that would be lovely. Come to the office and I'll make drinks.'

The others left, but Sue stayed put. 'Is she coming?' murmured Steph.

I peeped round the door. Sue was spinning on the spot, arms stretched wide, with an enormous grin on her face. 'She'll be with us shortly,' I whispered.

CHAPTER 16

Now that the Great Hall was free of its mysterious noises, our next task was to decide what to do about Nora and Superintendent Hicks. It wasn't that Steph and I didn't appreciate the seriousness of the situation, but Nora was cramping our style. Her comments on matters as diverse as what we had for breakfast through to my beauty routine and how we chose to spend our evenings were somewhat intrusive.

'What are we going to do?' muttered Steph, after Nora sailed through the bedroom door one evening and caught us kissing. Her face was a picture.

'I'll have a think,' I said, and poured us a glass of wine each to help.

Superintendent Hicks's behaviour doesn't make sense, I thought, taking a hefty sip. *He's nice to Nora now, but for years he wanted to get rid of her. From looking at her record, Nora hasn't changed – but the superintendent has. Why was he so mean to her?*

I mulled over the few times when men – and boys – had been mean to me. Not me and other women: specifically me. 'Oh!' I sat upright.

'What is it?' asked Steph crossly, putting down her glass and mopping at a splash of red wine on her top.

'I could be wrong,' I said, 'but I have a theory. I'll pop to the Bridewell tomorrow and test it out. Huw won't mind.'

'Whatever,' said Steph, getting up. 'I'll just get changed.'

The next day, I wasted no time in getting to the Bridewell. As soon as I let myself in, Superintendent Hicks rushed into the hall, pipe in hand. 'Where have you been? Why have you abandoned me? Where's Nora?' Suddenly, he looked worried.

'She's staying with Steph,' I said quickly. I didn't approve of the superintendent's actions, not at all, but I couldn't let him think the worst. 'She's cross with you, and she has reason to be.'

'Don't see why,' said the superintendent.

I walked over to the steps and sat down. 'Let me tell you a story, Superintendent. When I was at high school, one lad was persistently horrible to me. He'd call me names, try and trip me up, that sort of thing. No one else, just me. One day, when I'd had enough, I waited until none of his mates were around, grabbed him by the tie and pushed him up against the wall. He didn't know I did judo. "Tell me what's going on," I said, "or else." He tried to deny it, but I wasn't letting go. In the end, he told me that he fancied me and he wanted my attention. "Treat 'em mean, keep 'em keen," he said.'

Superintendent Hicks ran a finger round the inside of his collar.

'I told him that firstly, there were better ways to get my attention, and secondly, that I wasn't interested. I hadn't come out at that point, so I left it at that.'

The superintendent's face had turned a peculiar colour. 'That's an interesting story,' he said. 'Though I don't know why you're telling me.'

'I think you do,' I said quietly. 'The ghost we've been hunting at St George's Hall overheard something you said at the Bridewell a long, long time ago. You told another officer that you wanted to get rid of Nora. And the ghost told Nora.'

'Oh my—' Superintendent Hicks stared at me, jaw slack. Then he recovered himself. 'What was I supposed to do?' he demanded. 'How was I supposed to behave? I had a young wife and a child on the way and I was happy enough. Then Nora arrived, full of fun and life and as sharp as a tack. How could I resist her? I tried to ignore her, but she sought me out for advice.'

'You could have maintained a professional distance,' I commented.

'Can you maintain a professional distance from

Nora?'

I huffed quietly. 'You stitched her up.'

'And I regretted it, but she was overstepping the mark. She was neglecting her job and trying to be a detective – and we already had plenty of those. What if I'd let her carry on and she'd turned out a better detective than me? I had a family to think of.'

He stopped, and shook his head. 'I hated myself every time I was rude to her or about her,' he said. 'I wept when she died. Then she came back as a ghost and I knew I'd see her every working day until I retired.' He took a long pull on his pipe. 'When I died, I never expected to come here. And Nora, my nemesis, was here to greet me. We'll never be free of each other. Unless…'

He held up his hand and scrutinised it. It was transparent, but no more than usual. He let it fall to his side, then went to the stairs and sat down heavily beside me. 'I thought telling you might…'

'Might send you to your rest?' I smiled. 'Doesn't look like it. Maybe if you told Nora—'

'Absolutely not,' said the superintendent. 'Anything but that.'

'Well, you need to do something, or Nora won't ever return to the Bridewell. Not without us escorting her. And to be honest, Superintendent, Steph and I would like our private life back.'

The superintendent thought for some time. 'I'm

prepared to apologise for what I said.'

'I should think so. It had better be a good one, too.'

'I've missed Nora terribly,' he said. 'I've wondered what I would do if she was gone for ever.'

'Maybe you should concentrate on getting yourself back in Nora's good books, rather than worrying about things that may never be.'

'You're right.' He gazed ahead resolutely. 'If you bring her tonight, I'll do my very best.'

And to be fair, he had. Short of getting down on his knees, he couldn't have been more remorseful. Nora looked astonished, then smug, and finally respectful. 'Thank you, Superintendent,' she said. 'I accept your apology.' Of course, the superintendent soon composed himself, but I think he was pleased.

***

Around a week after our encounter with Ronald Ainscough at St George's Hall, Steph and I kept an evening appointment at the Bridewell.

Nora and Superintendent Hicks were waiting for us in the yard, with Prince and Queen Vic standing a few metres away, cropping invisible grass. I climbed halfway up the wrought-iron stairs, phone in hand. 'Are you ready?'

'Of course we're ready.' Nora clapped her hands. 'This is so exciting!'

'We know,' said Steph, with a grin.

I unlocked my phone and checked the signal. Two

and a half bars. 'OK, here we go.' I opened the email the Chief had sent to all staff and clicked on the article link. '*VALUABLE JEWELLERY FOUND IN ROOF OF ST GEORGE'S HALL*,' I read.

Nora squealed.

'*A remarkable discovery was made at St George's Hall on Monday. The planned repairs to the barrel-vaulted roof had been halted due to building issues, but when the expert restoration team began stripping one of the plaster panels, ready for repair, they found more than dust and spiders. Encased within the plaster was an emerald necklace valued at half a million pounds.*'

Superintendent Hicks whistled.

'*Inspector Frank Farnsworth of Merseyside Police, who has a particular interest in historic crime, led the investigation into the whereabouts of the necklace, which has a Victorian-style setting. Together with Adam Fagan, a long-standing employee of HMP Liverpool who is also an amateur historian, they identified it as having belonged to a Lady Huyton, from whom it was snatched during a concert at the Hall in 1896. Lady Huyton's family are delighted to have the necklace back. "We'd love to keep this piece of family treasure," said Sir John Huyton, "but given the cost of living, we'll probably sell it to finance roof repairs."*'

'From one roof to another,' said Steph.

'Chief Inspector Richard Strachan observed that it was deeply satisfying to employ staff with well-rounded interests and enable them to extend their policing role. "I couldn't be prouder of the team," he said.' I grinned at Steph. 'And that was how we got off the hook,' I told the ghosts.

'Well done, everyone,' said Superintendent Hicks.

'Yes, well done us,' said Nora. 'And the inspector, of course. Just think, if I hadn't had those strange visions, none of this would have come to light. I wonder what else we'll uncover in our investigations?'

Superintendent Hicks suddenly became very interested in his shoelaces.

'That can wait for another day,' I said. 'We haven't wrapped up this one yet.'

'Speaking of which,' said Nora, 'isn't that the inspector's car?'

Sure enough, a few seconds later Inspector Farnsworth's green Volvo pulled into view. The inspector wound down his window. 'Good evening,' he said, smiling. 'Do hurry up, we've got a ghost to find.'

It took us almost as long to lock up the Bridewell as it did to drive to St John's Gardens. The inspector pulled into a parking space outside the World Museum and put a note on the dashboard: *POLICE OFFICER ON DUTY*. 'You'll have to show me the way,' he said. 'Can someone grab the folder from the passenger-side door bucket, please?'

I waited for the superintendent to get out and obliged. 'Have you done more research, sir?'

'The nice thing about researching a notable family,' said Inspector Farnsworth, 'is that all the records are there.'

'Really?' asked Nora. 'How far have you got?'

'Quite some way,' said the inspector. 'But Mary should be first to hear it. Well, the good news.'

'Oh, of course,' said Nora. 'Come on everybody, don't stand there dawdling.'

As we entered the gardens, I wondered whether Mary would be there. What if the removal of Ronald Ainscough, and therefore the ghost hunters, had been enough to send her to her rest? But as we climbed up the hill I saw a figure in a loose gown ahead of me, wandering along the paths and singing to herself.

'Lavender's blue, diddle diddle

Lavender's green,

When I am king, diddle diddle

You shall be queen…'

'Mary!' I called, and she turned. 'We have news for you!'

Mary's expression, which was alarmed at first – possibly because there were more of us than usual and we were a mixed company – became joyful. 'You have news of my treasure? Of Thomas?'

'We do, Miss Sweeney,' said the inspector. 'My

name is Mr Farnsworth, and I specialise in finding lost families.'

I grinned and nudged Steph, who gave me a stern look.

Mary hurried towards us, running the last few steps in her eagerness. 'Well, tell me then!'

Inspector Farnsworth opened his folder. 'First of all, your baby *was* named Thomas – Thomas John Henry Sweeney. Your cousin Thomas and his wife Emily brought him up.'

'Oh yes, Thomas and Emily wanted children, but somehow it never happened,' said Mary, with rather a superior air.

'Thomas was sent to Eton for schooling, then Oxford University, and he became an envoy and later, an ambassador. He lived in all sorts of places – Italy, Greece, Norway – and he married and had six children.'

'Six?' cried Mary. 'I have six grandchildren? Tell me their names, pray!'

'Let's sit down,' said Inspector Farnsworth, moving to a nearby bench. 'I have a great deal to tell you…'

At first, Steph and I tried to keep back our tears, but soon we were crying openly. Luckily, the gardens were deserted apart from us, for who knows what anyone would have thought. Nora was nearly as bad, and the superintendent offered her his handkerchief more than once, but she shook her head, gripping the bench as if she might float away otherwise.

'I must be dreaming,' murmured Mary. 'Six grandchildren, eighteen great grandchildren and – how many great-great-grandchildren did you say?'

'I've found forty so far,' said Inspector Farnsworth. 'There are great-great-great grandchildren, too.'

'Good heavens,' said Mary, and her voice shook. 'I cannot believe it. I never thought I would find my baby, but all this? It is too much.' Suddenly, her voice was weaker. 'I do not deserve to be so happy.'

'Yes, you do,' I said. 'You did nothing wrong.'

Mary nodded. 'The attendants said I could not help my nature.'

'You did nothing wrong,' I repeated. 'Now you can be happy.'

The bench was visible through Mary's body. 'I just wish I might see my Thomas.' The last word was barely more than breath.

'You will,' said the inspector, 'I'm sure of it.' But Mary was gone before he could finish his sentence.

I buried my head in Steph's shoulder. 'I'm happy, really,' I choked out. And I was. Mary had found her treasure. Having almost lost mine, I didn't plan on making that mistake again.

'I'm happy too,' Steph said, between sniffles.

'Well,' said the inspector, 'another case resolved.' He sounded rather sad. 'What next?'

'Going home,' said Steph and I, together.

'Yes,' said Inspector Farnsworth. 'I've had to tell a couple of fibs to my wife to join you tonight, and I'd better get home before my cover's blown. I'll drop you on the way.'

Steph took my hand as we walked to the car. We made for the Bridewell to drop off Nora and the superintendent, who were all smiles now, and then Inspector Farnsworth took us to Steph's apartment.

'Tasha,' said Steph, as we watched the Volvo drive away.

'Yes?' I looked down at her.

'I know we're working tomorrow, and we've only just got the apartment to ourselves again, and there's probably stuff we should talk over…'

I wondered where this was going. 'Yes?'

'But I think we should get changed, head out and see where the evening takes us.'

I squeezed her hand. 'Best thing I've heard all day.'

WHAT TO READ NEXT

Hopefully you won't have to wait too long for the next Spirit of the Law adventure, as I already have ideas bubbling in my brain! But in the meantime...

If you enjoy light mystery with more than a touch of magic, try my Magical Bookshop series. The first book is *Every Trick in the Book*, and can be found at http://mybook.to/bookshop1 (global link).

If you liked the creepy, spooky nature of this book, you might like my series of Halloween Sherlock novelettes, which are fairly traditional in nature and have a similar atmosphere. The first in series is *The Case of the Snow-White Lady*: http://mybook.to/SnowWhiteLady (global link).

However, if you enjoy contemporary mysteries in a village setting, you could give the Booker and Fitch Mysteries a go (I write this series with Paula Harmon). The first one is *Murder for Beginners*: https://mybook.to/Beginners.

ACKNOWLEDGEMENTS

As always, my first thanks go to my super beta readers – Carol Bissett, Ruth Cunliffe, Paula Harmon and Stephen Lenhardt – and my long-suffering proofreader, John Croall. Thank you so much for your help! Any errors that remain are of course my responsibility.

If you've read the previous books in the series, you'll know that the Bridewell is a real building: Bridewell Studios and Gallery, which I visited on a Heritage Open Day (https://www.bridewellstudiosliverpool.org). St George's Hall is also very much a real building, which you can take a tour of, and the staff were lovely on the day I visited (though I didn't ask any questions about ghosts). You can find out more about this marvellous building here: https://www.stgeorgeshallliverpool.co.uk/. St John's Gardens are also real, as is Liverpool Central Library: prepare to be wowed by both the modern building and the Picton Library.

As in the previous book, I consulted several maps of Liverpool, and a list is here: https://liverpool1207blog.wordpress.com/old-liverpool-maps/.

As an interesting footnote, when Mary sings 'Lavender's Blue', it isn't quite the innocent nursery rhyme we know. Here is an article on the original lyrics: https://randombitsoffascination.com/2017/05/09/the-shocking-lyrics-of-lavenders-blue/

And of course, many thanks to you, dear reader! I hope you've enjoyed the Bridewell team's latest adventure. If you have, please consider leaving a short review or a rating on Amazon and/or Goodreads. Reviews and ratings are very important to authors, as they help books to find new readers.

COVER CREDITS

Image (cropped and coloured): St George's Hall by SomeDriftwood at https://flickr.com/photos/arthurjohnpicton/5027224982/ (public domain).

Cover font: IM FELL Great Primer Pro by Igino Marini: https://www.fontsquirrel.com/fonts/im-fell-great-primer-pro. License: SIL Open Font License v1.10: http://scripts.sil.org/OFL.

ABOUT THE AUTHOR

Liz Hedgecock grew up in London, England, did an English degree, and then took forever to start writing. After several years working in the National Health Service, some short stories crept into the world. A few even won prizes. Then the stories started to grow longer…

Now Liz travels between the nineteenth and twenty-first centuries, murdering people. To be fair, she does usually clean up after herself.

Liz's reimaginings of Sherlock Holmes, the Magical Bookshop series, her Pippa Parker cozy mystery series, the Booker & Fitch and Caster & Fleet mystery series (with Paula Harmon), and the Maisie Frobisher Mysteries are available in ebook and paperback.

Liz lives in Cheshire with her husband and two sons, and when she's not writing or child-wrangling you can usually find her reading, messing about on

Twitter, or cooing over stuff in museums and art galleries. That's her story, anyway, and she's sticking to it.

Website/blog: http://lizhedgecock.wordpress.com
Facebook: http://www.facebook.com/lizhedgecockwrites
Twitter: http://twitter.com/lizhedgecock
Goodreads: https://www.goodreads.com/lizhedgecock

BOOKS BY LIZ HEDGECOCK

To check out my books, please visit my Amazon author page: http://author.to/LizH (global link). If you follow me there, you'll be notified when I release a new book.

The Magical Bookshop (6 novels)
An eccentric owner, a hostile cat, and a bookshop with a mind of its own. Can Jemma turn around the second-worst secondhand bookshop in London? And can she learn its secrets?

Pippa Parker Mysteries (6 novels)
Meet Pippa Parker: mum, amateur sleuth, and resident of a quaint English village called Much Gadding. And then the murders began…

Booker & Fitch Mysteries (5 novels, with Paula Harmon)
Jade Fitch hopes for a fresh start when she opens a

new-age shop in a picturesque market town. Meanwhile, Fi Booker runs a floating bookshop as well as dealing with her teenage son. And as soon as they meet, it's murder…

Caster & Fleet Mysteries (6 novels, with Paula Harmon)

There's a new detective duo in Victorian London – and they're women! Meet Katherine and Connie, two young women who become partners in crime. Solving it, that is!

Mrs Hudson & Sherlock Holmes (3 novels)

Mrs Hudson is Sherlock Holmes's elderly landlady. Or is she? Find out her real story here.

Maisie Frobisher Mysteries (4 novels)

When Maisie Frobisher, a bored young Victorian socialite, goes travelling in search of adventure, she finds more than she could ever have dreamt of. Mystery, intrigue and a touch of romance.

The Spirit of the Law (3 novellas)

Meet a detective duo – a century apart! A modern-day police constable and a hundred-year-old ghost team up to solve the coldest of cases.

Sherlock & Jack (3 novellas)

Jack has been ducking and diving all her life. But

when she meets the great detective Sherlock Holmes they form an unlikely partnership. And Jack discovers that she is more important than she ever realised…

Tales of Meadley (2 novelettes)
A romantic comedy mini-series based in the village of Meadley, with a touch of mystery too.

Halloween Sherlock (3 novelettes)
Short dark tales of Sherlock Holmes and Dr Watson, perfect for a grim winter's night.

For children
A Christmas Carrot (with Zoe Harmon)
Perkins the Halloween Cat (with Lucy Shaw)
Rich Girl, Poor Girl (for 9-12 year olds)

Printed in Great Britain
by Amazon